The Vanishing Hours

www.**penguin**.co.uk

The Vanishing Hours

Barney Norris

doubleday

TRANSWORLD PUBLISHERS
61–63 Uxbridge Road, London W5 5SA
www.penguin.co.uk

Transworld is part of the Penguin Random House group of companies
whose addresses can be found at global.penguinrandomhouse.com

Penguin
Random House
UK

First published in Great Britain in 2019 by Doubleday
an imprint of Transworld Publishers

A CIP catalogue record for this book
is available from the British Library

ISBN 9780857525710

Typeset in 11.5/14.71 pt Adobe Garamond
by Integra Software Services Pvt. Ltd, Pondicherry

Printed and bound in Great Britain by Clays Ltd, Elcograf S.p.A.

Penguin Random House is committed to a sustainable
future for our business, our readers and our planet. This book
is made from Forest Stewardship Council® certified paper.

1 3 5 7 9 10 8 6 4 2

Millions are condemned to a stiller doom than mine, and millions are in silent revolt against their lot. Nobody knows how many rebellions besides political rebellions ferment in the masses of life which people earth.

Charlotte Brontë, *Jane Eyre*

For Charlie

One

Poor folk mun get on as they can.

Charlotte Brontë, *Jane Eyre*

THIS IS NOT my real life and I don't think now that it ever will be. It is probably time for me to accept that my real life will never happen. It would need to have started already to have any chance of lasting much more than a moment, of growing into anything. I should content myself with having this much instead.

I can never eat much before the appointments. Too apprehensive. I sat in the kitchen looking out of the window at my square of back garden, and drank a cup of decaf tea. I don't go anywhere near caffeine now. Breakfast was a piece of toast with butter and strawberry jam. I supposed it was breakfast – it might just as easily have been lunch. Afterwards I left my plate and my cup unwashed by the sink, and went into the garden, and inspected the woodbine, and inspected the rose. There was a frost last night. Is the woodbine in the right kind of pot for it to make it through the winter? I spent more time over the rose. A month ago, I cut it back to its very base when the last of the leaves died, because it had been sprawling all over the place for years. Will that have worked? Did I go too far? I will have to wait till spring to find out, but all the same I watch for signs, I watch for clues of what's going to happen.

ROSE. Something that dies. Something that needs to be cut down to nothing from time to time. Something that lives twice, in summer and autumn. A smell like a memory, black spot always nipping at the leaves.

The masterpiece I thought I was going to weave into the world would have been an encyclopedia of every word I'd ever fallen in love with. It would have been the climax of the Open University degree I started working towards when they told me I was well into the swing of my latest recovery. The fifteenth or sixteenth attempt I made of starting again. It went the way of all the others, before and since. There have been so many now, life after life that never happened; almost seventy years of dreams that came and went, and another birthday crawling closer as I turn steadily into the old woman I never believed I'd be. But I would have liked to write my encyclopedia. Of all the dreams I never made happen, I'm sorriest about that one being stillborn.

I wanted to do something for people who had forgotten that the world, as well as being a terrible and frightening and dark place to spend time in, was also filled with things worth remembering. Things that anyone would be glad to have seen and done. I thought if I could record all the beauty that I had witnessed, every image that had made me feel like my days were worth having, then maybe others in the same kind of dark would be encouraged to look at their own lives differently too, to see past the things that beset them and look out for beauty. I would have loved to have found a book like that while I was deepest down in my own trouble.

People would be able to read it like a dictionary, from A to Z, but also to follow other paths through it, other stories, if they chose. Because that's the way you fall in love with things – they don't just come at you one after the other; they sidle up, reach you slantwise. Days worth living fall on us like the sun coming in through windows, making unexpected angles. That is how I've met the words I've loved. I wanted to capture the fact that things aren't only beautiful in their own right – they're beautiful because of what they've meant to people, and what they mean to you. So this would be an encyclopedia you could get lost in, with every entry cross-referencing to other entries, so that you could wander through everything beautiful that the author had ever encountered, take whatever path you fancied, and never leave, if you didn't want to.

Not much of the draft I prepared survives now, but I can show you how it would have worked.

> *APPLE. When I was young I went with my family on a holiday to WALES, and while we were there we climbed up a mountain. When we got to the top, DAD took some apples from his rucksack and we ate one each. I took a few bites of mine till it looked like the kind of apple you see in the Snow White film, and then I threw the core away. My uncle became suddenly angry with me. He asked me why I had thrown away the apple when I'd barely eaten half of it, after my dad had taken the trouble to carry it all the way up to the top of this mountain. He didn't understand why I'd be so careless after all that trouble. At the time I was upset, but ever since that day I have eaten every bit of an apple, leaving nothing but the stalk and the pips and the last of the core, and every time I finish an apple I think of my dad, the trouble he took for me, the things he carried to help me out.*

> *DAD. [This would be a long entry in the full book, but I will sketch a shorter story here.] I don't have as many*

memories of my dad as I would like, but I can tell you about the DANCING TREE. When I was small, MUM and Dad would take us out for walks in the woods near where we lived, to visit the Dancing Tree. Dad always walked too fast, so I couldn't keep up with him and had to break into little jog-trots. But for as long as I could keep up, he used to like to tell me little stories. He would teach me the history of the WARS OF THE ROSES, for example, and tell me about kings who had risen and fallen right where we were walking now in times gone by. In this way I learned many beautiful things that no one else knew at the school I went to, and I felt proud, because keeping up with Dad had made me special; it had given me access to secrets that made the world bigger than it had been before.

DANCING TREE, THE. In the middle of the woods near our house was a tree that looked like we had caught it dancing. Its branches twisted and turned in such a way that it seemed to be trying to get away from itself, or move along to some MUSIC that had stopped just moments before we got there. We thought the tree stayed very still in its ridiculous pose in the hope that we wouldn't notice it and laugh at it, and that we might leave it alone. But we saw it, all right, and used to like to dance beneath it, especially when there were LEAVES in autumn that we could kick up in the air.

LATIN. I never properly learned Latin, but at school the way I found to be popular was to be good at acting, and that meant I had a reputation as a good speaker. The Latin teacher got to hear about my control of Shakespearean verse, which I think was good for my age, and asked me to compete in an inter-school Latin-speaking competition that was being held across the county. I entered, and won the competition, though I had no idea what I was saying except that it was by Pliny and it was about a town. But I liked the feeling of winning enough that I entered the competition once more the following year, and was delighted to retain my title.

LEAVES. When I finished school I moved to the city, and when I married my husband it was there we made our home. At that time, in the year after my marriage, I became very conscious of not having come from that environment, and not feeling at home there. London in the eighties was a place of dust and buses, engines like hornets everywhere, elderly men who walked the pavements while the pubs shut for lunch as if they were on patrol; thin men, their clothes held up sometimes with belts of rope and string, and for a young woman who didn't belong to that world, it seemed very alien.

For the first time, I became interested in the world where I had grown up at a conscious level. Throughout my childhood, I had simply lived; I'd never really thought about what I was doing. Now I started to collect books about the natural world. I wanted to identify more consciously with having come from the wild. The first challenge I set myself was to learn the names and shapes of the leaves that one might come across on trees in England. I would look at pictures in books and memorise the English and LATIN names, then go to parks and test myself. I wasn't working at that time. I was looking for a job and looking after my husband while he went to work and we decided whether or not to start a family, and the leaves became my happiest project then. I felt like I caught glimpses in among them of the person I wanted to be.

MUSIC. [This again would be a very long entry. I will just touch on one aspect of it here.] I never enjoyed my music lessons at school, but I kept doing them because what I did love was performing in concerts. I got quite good at the violin so I was allowed to play in the school orchestra. What I found intoxicating was the way that performing long pieces there reminded me of the THEATRE, my favourite place of all. There was the same sense of telling a story, of spinning feelings out of thin air. That taught me something important about the theatre, actually. I learned that it wasn't the words actors said that audiences listened to, just as people didn't really listen to the notes played by musicians. What everyone is listening for all the time is the thing beneath that, the real thing, the feelings that another person is feeling just a heartbeat away from you. I used to like that vivid feeling of entering into a game with the audience of mums and dads who were listening, where we would try to move them, and they would listen to these things we chose to play, but half an hour after we had finished, no one would be able to tell that the game had ever happened. All the music would have disappeared as if it had never existed. That was the joy of the gossamer game of trying to share a feeling with another person – that none of it was real, you couldn't put your finger on any part of it, so it all felt like a secret you were sharing.

THEATRE. The first theatre I remember visiting was a place for children somewhere at the edge of London. I was only very young, and my eyes hadn't yet seen very many things, so I couldn't see where the set was hinged together, or where the paint needed touching up. I couldn't see the bored usher waiting at the back to count us all out at the end again – anything like that was invisible to me. I only remember this woman, her face wide in amazement, taking us through a forest of tall trees and introducing us to the animals there.

WALES. We always used to take our holidays in Wales. What I remember most of all is a New Year we celebrated in a converted pigsty up near Conwy, where the world's best ice cream is sold just off the quay. It was freezing and we wore our pyjamas under our clothes all day. No one has that kind of holiday any more – everywhere has central heating – and I miss the campfire, the making do, the shivering teeth, the cups of tea and raisin porridge. I didn't make it to New Year that evening, but I did stay up late, playing a board game with my parents that was based on the WARS OF THE ROSES.

WARS OF THE ROSES, THE. A few months after DAD had taught me the story of the Wars of the Roses, he took me on a very special trip to the site of the Battle of Naseby. There was nothing much to see, but I felt very close to the people I had learned about, standing in the place where some of them had died. Dad took a photo of me standing there, and on the way home in the car we ate an APPLE.

You can see how my encyclopedia would have worked, and how quickly it would have proliferated and flowered and grown a thousand heads, become a huge and overwhelming chorus of stories about the beautiful world, the beautiful words. I thought if someone were willing to publish it then it might do people good. But as I said, the work was never completed. The Open University told me it wasn't a legitimate academic activity. But it had become too important to me for me to be willing to write anything else. If I couldn't do that project, I decided I'd rather do nothing at all. So I withdrew from the degree, and abandoned the work.

I often think that, had I found strength to complete the encyclopedia, to gather together a lifetime's words and wonderings, the truth of my story would become clearer than any list of facts and dates and places. It would have been a way of seeing to the heart of me, so people could have looked beyond the smallness of the facts and glimpsed the secret truth that my life felt big too, under the surface. My days felt unique to me. That's a harder thing to convey when I say only that I was born at the start of the fifties, was old enough to see all the excitements of the decade that followed but too young to take part in them; that my childhood and youth in the backwater country meant I carried on singing in a church choir long after I realised I didn't believe in God, and missed out entirely on the pleasures of punk and 1976, though it was my generation who made it; that I got away to London when I could, when I was finished with home economics classes and honouring my mother and father, but that the experiment of making my way in the big world failed and before long I found myself drifting back into the west, to a series of small jobs – secretarial work at a college, then at a dentist's, followed by a move to the complaints counter of a supermarket because the regular hours of those other jobs had become too tiring. The occasional breakdown when things got too much for me. And the purchase of this bungalow a decade ago, and all the time alone in it, no one to share it with. What does that list show you of the heart of a person? Even if I shared what I did with my spare time – the reading of Emily Dickinson poems, painting by numbers, jigsaws, a little crochet, once or twice a year a trip to London to hear a band play somewhere – that still doesn't touch the sides of what it really felt like. All of the containers we pour our lives into seem so small, when you set them against the feeling of being, the way the light hit you, the way things struck you when you stared out of a window in the mornings. It takes something more ingenious to let anyone into what that was like. That would have been my encyclopedia.

ASYLUM. A shelter from violence. A place of rest. A way of hiding. An act of charity. Understanding passed from one person to another. A place where people are given permission to believe in the seriousness of their predicaments, the importance and onceness of their lives, and not to talk themselves down, not to deflect sympathy or medical attention, not to disappear under the weight of stories the newspapers would rather cover. A place where people are told that they deserve to grieve, to hurt, to heal. A place where those who cannot heal will at least be looked after, so that they can still experience slow life as its petals fall, one meal, one breath, one glass of cold water drained down the throat after another, as the simple beauty of rain on glass or walking in the dawn reveals itself, morning after morning, even to those who will always have to suffer to be able to enjoy the glories they are given.

In the garden, the blessing I find is that I don't have to think. I can be a living and a breathing thing, like the honeysuckle, like the rose. And like them, no more is required of me; I need not speak, nor think about anything at all. We are all simply taking in the light. In the summer I watch how the stems grow, and in the winter I look for the way that things die back, and all of the phantoms that attend our human lives, the fevers and imaginings, those go away for as long as I'm watching. No one talks to me out there. No one asks for anything.

It was cold today though, so once I'd been over the rose and seen there was no rot setting in, I went back inside, shivering. Old lady now, or soon enough. I suppose that was why I was feeling the cold. Soon it will be time for my bus pass. But I've learned things from hanging around so long. I've learned how to find peace in the garden, for one thing. And I've learned enough to know it would snow today, before the radio told me – I'd seen the signs for myself. In the garden, I could feel the day clearing space for its show, its dance, its dazzle. The temperature dropping to prepare the ground.

I went back inside and saw my breakfast things by the sink, and sighed, and went and washed them up. I ran the hot tap till it stung the back of my hand, then put the plug in and squeezed a bit of Fairy into the sink. I scrubbed the plate and the knife and the cup with the washing-up brush, then rinsed them under the tap that was still running and put them on the drainer. Then I picked up a tea towel and dried each object, and put them back in their rightful places in the correct drawers and cupboards. I watched the garden through the window all the time I worked, and was rewarded not just by its stillness and silence, but by the arrival of a robin, who hopped down from the holly tree in the corner and made his murderous, tentative way across the lawn. I wondered whether he thought I'd left him something. Perhaps I should have done. I returned the clean cutlery to the drawer and stepped back to survey the kitchen, shipshape again. It was almost as if I'd never been there. When I looked back out of the window, the robin had gone.

I used to have cats, and they would leave the bodies of birds and other small creatures strewn over the lawn. The worst was after snowfall, when the fate of a robin or some other poor creature was marked in bright blood against the snow. I would wake and look into the garden – sometimes it was still dark and sometimes I would get up after the sun had risen – and there would be the blood on the white snow, the head of a robin or the head of some other bird lying some distance from the rest of what was left. In daylight the colours were almost beautiful – the red and white, and the roiled snow where the cat had danced the bird to death. I wouldn't want to have a cat around now. They're murderers really, only ever a moment from cruelty.

I went back into the dark of the hall and to my room to prepare for the day, and as I walked I was seized again by memory.

WATERWORN. Something bruised out of the form it had before. Something that has lost its shape. Something beautiful that you wouldn't think you could find in nature, a shape you could hardly believe in. Something distorted. A shape like a memory that's ebbing into silence. A shape that you want to run over your tongue. Something damaged. Something that will one day disappear. Something that used to be more than it is now. Something that has seen things. Something that has travelled, that has been rolled across the bottom of the ocean. The way that hope runs out.

When I was a girl I used to dive all the time into remembering the day Dad walked out on us. The memory was like a stone I carried in my pocket, and I would run my finger and my thumb over its surface all the day, wearing it smooth, fitting its shape to my skin till I felt it might be part of me. I liked to think it was a dark blue coldness, that stone I loved but never could take out and see. I wondered whether everyone carried one of their own around with them, a memory they turned into the centre of themselves, tucked into a secret pocket on the hidden inside of their raincoat, holding them together, weighing them down.

I wanted so much for that secret stone to be part of my body. Have you ever done that trick, when you place the index finger of your right hand against the index finger of your left in front of your eyes, then look past them both into the middle distance, and find all of a sudden a trick of the eye is showing you a third stump of finger suspended in between the first two, like a little Christmas sausage? And then when you try to look straight at your fingers again, you find it's gone. I wanted Dad to be like that – there all the time, waiting to be with me, even though I couldn't see him.

All the best children's books have a secret compartment. A way of getting into a different world, a little doorway out of the bedroom where you're reading. Like the secret at the top of the Faraway Tree, the miracle that took those children every time they climbed out into a different world. Sometimes it's a clock chiming or sometimes a tree or a puddle or a post box; it might be any ordinary thing, but there will be something magical about the book if the book's worth reading. It will take you somewhere else. Perhaps that's because growing up is a kind of exile, of being kicked out of the moment when everything seemed possible. Perhaps that's why children's books have more trapdoors than the books we read as adults. All the trapdoors in all the children's books in the world are ways of dreaming your way back into that time when you took the world at face value, and nothing had ever been lost.

I was dressed and ready to head out. A vest top and two T-shirts, a cardigan and a jumper over that, and then my big raincoat that gives me the padded shape of a snowman. You have to take staying warm enough seriously in these Salisbury Plain winters. From the basket by the door I picked up a hat and a scarf and gloves as well. For a moment I turned to look back at the house again before I left it, through the dark hallway to the light in the kitchen and a glimpse of the garden and happiness beyond. I always like my home best when it feels like no one lives there. When it's totally empty and silent. It may sound strange, but I love to imagine the rooms when I'm away from them, nothing moving, just dust settling slowly in the bars of light that strafe each corner of the room over the course of each spinning day.

I opened the front door and picked up my car keys and headed out into the morning. The yellow rose climbing the front of the house was over now; there'd be no more flowers on it till the spring. When I arrived here ten years ago, the first things I planted were climbers and vines; woodbine and nightshade and jasmine and roses up the walls. I wanted to turn my world all green, all green. A burying of leaves and a cloud of scents foamy as shampoo all around me in the summer. Beautiful hiding places for the birds and for me.

INTERLUDE. A moment of exile. A time that passes between one game and another. A moment spent indoors before you go back out to play. A moment spent outdoors before you go back to the party. A breath. A possibility. A time spent thinking.

As a girl, I was always in love with the dream of a life in which Dad never left us. So I used to look everywhere for the secret routes out of the everyday, and that was how I came to obsess over that morning in the way I did. I wanted to go over the memory of it again and again, to try to get the last pictures I had of Dad right. There was nothing ever so special about what I saw that morning, but all the same I wanted with all of my heart to hold on to what I remembered, the last little glimpses of him.

So I burnished those memories time and again, the beads on a rosary I made from my life, and made my own religion, and kept it all secret from my mum and from anyone, kept it all for myself. If I could remember the way it all happened, perhaps there would be a part of me that never changed, never fell away from him like the cliffs that crumble into the sea. Perhaps there would be a tiny piece of me that could live with him for ever, a wish that endured long after the hope of being picked up in his arms again had faded, long after it had become absurd to imagine he was alive and somehow still looking like he did that morning when he walked away. Because girls do love their fathers. Especially if they never really get a chance to know them. Then their fathers are perfect, and the rest of the world will become only echoes and shadows of the first man they loved.

Strange, how every year the newspapers have told me the planet is getting warmer, but my world tends to seem a little more Arctic with each turn of the year, each calendar dropped in the recycling bin. The bloom of things always seems to be fading, but then I am of a melancholic disposition, always have been. I look out for the way things dwindle. Every morning, I'm in the garden going over the woodbine leaves to look for rot. Even in the spring of my life, as a young woman in London, I would go out into the garden and water the plants, and snip away the side leaves of tomato plants so they would fruit more, and I would look for the signs of death. The withering of cuttings in their pots, the black spot on leaves, the vines that had snapped in the wind, the branch of a tree that stayed barren when the spring came. Always, I went into the garden expecting death. When I went for coffee with a friend, sometimes on the way home on the bus I'd catch myself wondering, how many more times will we meet like that? How many more times are our paths going to cross? I never thought of it as a bad thing. Just the way things work. We are given very little time and it runs out on us. Two lives can only intertwine so often in the years they have.

Negative, yes, the manifestation of a depressive tendency, but that was who I was, and in the end I think that fearfulness protected me a little. It made things easier when I gave up London and came back to Wiltshire to spend my summer years – and now to begin my autumn – out of the way here where no one really knows me. I had thought it might happen all along, that failure, that surrender, that return. When I made the move, I said to myself: this was always a possibility, this flight back to the margins. And that insulated me a little, I think, from the shock of heading home, and settling for a smaller life, and making less noise than I'd hoped to.

I read not long ago that PTSD sufferers seem to pass on a worry gene to their children. The children of holocaust survivors, for example, all had abnormally high amounts of some gene that made them more risk averse, more cautious. And I thought, when I read that, how sensible, that those who've been through trouble would seek, even at the deepest level, even in the genes they pass on to their kids, to protect them from the harm they'd seen. What love there is in people – far beyond consciousness – in those genes passed on from damaged parents to their children.

I don't know whether my parents ever went through any event so terrible that they passed on a sense of the onceness of things to me. If they did, Mum never talked about it. Both of them lived through the war, of course, but they were too young to get involved with it all, so I don't know what they saw from the seclusion of the Plain. In her old age Mum never shared any stories, never believed hers were important or interesting enough to share. I too have battled with the same creeping conviction – that my own stories are too unremarkable to share. But it's not true. It's just that we've been taught to value some more than others.

At the edge of the village, I saw that someone had run over a cat and left it entrailed by the roadside, and almost had to pull over to let the pang of grief pass. It made me want to be sick, to see the way its body had been splayed open, head crushed on the road. It must have been hiding behind a parked car, and startled at the sound of an engine, and run out at the last moment, nothing to be done. That was how it always happened, that last-minute sprint to death, and no braking distance in the world able to save you. I wondered who it was who had not stopped, who'd driven on without checking whether the body was wearing a collar. Perhaps it was easier to flee the scene, pretend it had never happened. That was easier than stopping and getting out of the car, and walking back, and looking at what you'd done. I wondered whether I should stop and look for a collar myself. It probably belonged to someone I knew – there were so few people living round here. But what would I do, scoop it up and carry it to someone's doorway? Bury it in a field so they didn't get to say goodbye? And what if I got there and the cat had no collar after all, and then I'd just have to walk away from it once more and get back in the car, having put myself through the sight of its death, its destruction? I drove on. It was easier, in the end, not to do anything – it normally is. Whenever it's humanly possible, people will look away. And that's part of survival as well, I suppose, of self-protection – the less admirable part of it.

I tried to shut my heart to the thought of one of my own neighbours wondering when they had last seen their cat, going out into the garden to call for it. Perhaps an indoor cat that had crept out, longing to hunt, unaccustomed to the road. What would they do when they found it? How would they pick up the pieces splayed out so red and sad? And was it another neighbour, I wondered, who had done it, who would have to drive past the scene of the death later today, and live with themselves all evening till the sharp freshness of the guilt fades, and try to get to sleep? If I were to go for a walk down the street of my village tonight at midnight, I thought, and there were two lights on, then I would have found the owner and the killer as easy as that. The two souls left sleepless by what had happened on the road. I rounded a bend, and the body was out of sight.

I'd never intended to climb as far as I did inside the memory of the day my father disappeared. It just happened, and I found, to begin with, I felt more alive when I thought about what used to happen than when things were actually happening to me. I wondered if I had the world the right way round. Because wouldn't you think it was real life that made you feel the most deeply? Wouldn't you guess that was true?

It seems a great robbery to me that the short time we get to explore consciousness and the short time we get to explore the world are falling always away from us at the same speed, and happening at once, like two rivers that have woven themselves endlessly together gone singsonging over a single cliff. It can make it difficult to tell one from the other, to find the point where you end and the world begins. It would surely be kinder to us all if there were a way of experiencing consciousness for a while without the complication of the rest of the world, and likewise to experience living in the world for a bit without any consciousness, before we got started on trying to sing the two songs at the same time. Without that, it stands to reason that we'll have a fight on our hands to keep things from blurring together.

The more time I spent thinking about the disappearance of my father, the more I noticed that everything around me in the real world, the world I could pick up and hold, started reminding me of things that had happened before. It seemed like every street I walked down was just a procession of quotations from other afternoons, call-backs to jokes I'd heard that morning, not a street in its own right. I started to lose the trick of just looking at one thing for its own sake. Whenever I talked to someone, a child or a grown-up, I thought only of all the people I'd known who they reminded me of. I couldn't hear what they were saying, or respond to them, without feeding my thoughts through every voice I'd ever heard before, like water seeping sorrowful up through sand-stone. Gradually, I realised the brain I seemed to feed everything through was Dad's. Everyone I talked to reminded me of him, and every conversation I had, I felt like it was really me and him talking. I always wondered what he might think or say wherever I was, and whatever was happening. And I started to wonder, as I let this sink in, whether the real world really existed after all. Every person I spent any time with started to seem like nothing more than a mask for my father, like a different draft of that first person I had lost and had to shine up all bright in the memory like a conker in the chestnut-smelling autumn.

I thought I saw the answer the first time I clapped eyes on a sloth in Regent's Park zoo. I watched the sloth as he slept hanging from his tree, and felt sure I'd seen the secret of the real shape of the world. The sloth sleeps for nearly twenty hours a day. He wakes to feed and drink, and then goes back to sleep again. I watched his gangly body in repose and felt certain that sloths knew something people had forgotten. That our real lives were our dream lives, the scenes we played out in our minds. The world was only a place that we visited to refuel for our dreaming. We were only really awake when we'd fallen asleep. Real life hides in hanging from a branch, and closing your eyes, and watching the pictures bleed into one another, like shapes in a coal fire, flickering, budding, burning.

PARADISE. A place that we visit in sleep. A dream people cling to by way of compensation. A journey someone hopes to go on one day. Something you remember, years later, and realise you didn't love enough at the time it was happening to you. Youth, once it's far enough behind you to look at it clearly.

So I'll tell the story of my last day with Dad.

I'm seven. I don't know how tall this means I am; the door where we pencilled in our heights as the years passed was lost long ago, I suppose, repainted the moment the next family moved in. The little markings a family makes to stake out the bounds of their lives shine so brightly to the people who see themselves reflected there, but they rarely matter to anyone else. They paint over the old lines and make new ones that mean completely different things to completely different people, even though, to a stranger, the two sets of lines marked against the same door frame and separated only by the coat of paint they're drawn on might look to be scrabbling away from the lino in perfect imitations of each other.

I'm seven, and lying in my bed, and I wake up like I usually do, with the light on my face because Mum has come in and she's thrown back the curtains. They're spaceship curtains, chosen by my brother because he had this room first. I want new ones, of

21

course, even though they're really nice curtains, because these are my brother's. But we haven't done anything about it yet because of how tight money is. At every dinner, this is one of the side dishes served. We get water in a jug on the table, and salt and pepper, and a talk Mum and Dad give each other about money and worrying. I know that means I have to put up with the spacemen.

I open my eyes all crossly, because that's how I always start, scrunching up my face because the day's being really bright, really full of itself, and I can see Mum silhouetted by the window with the trees peeking in over her shoulder like a lot of nosey monkeys.

'Wakey wakey, rise and shine!'

'I don't want to.'

'Come on, little one.'

I remember crisp as ice the bed I am lying in. A single bed made of pine and varnished till it looks orange. I like best of all to lie with my teeth against the top of the headboard, and feel how smooth it is to bite it and leave little marks behind me, like the scars grooved on hillsides by glaciers long ago. This means there are quite a lot of bite marks at both ends of my bed. The duvet is a warm yellow snail-shell around me, or otherwise I feel like the yolk in an egg, and I'm all balled up in it as happy as my body can be. I always sleep on my left-hand side in this room, which means looking out towards the window. As an adult, I've found that it's not so much the side I sleep on that matters to me, but facing the best source of light.

Now Mum says, 'I'll get the breakfast things out and I'll see you downstairs in a minute.'

'All right.'

Mum smiles then, and comes over to me, and strokes my hair with her hand that is enchanted with rings on each finger celebrating the sunlight, and gives me a kiss on the forehead, and of course I don't feel cross at her any more for waking me up because she's nice, and it's nice that she likes me. I can tell that she likes me because of her smile, which I see very clearly as she straightens up and away from me, then turns and walks out of the bedroom.

Then it's action stations, and I have to get out of bed and into my dressing gown and out of the room before I hear the kettle boiling, because that means I've been quick. And it is here in the story I'm telling that I am almost overwhelmed, as the feeling fills me of being a girl of seven once again, and of leaping from bed because the world is beautiful and I want to drink up every drop of it, and of knowing Mum and Dad will be downstairs when I get there, and that they will both love me, and they will both smile when they see my face.

This memory is like a scab that I can't help picking, the telling of it an addiction I can't control.

Out of bed, I reach up and take down my pink dressing gown from the back of the door and pull it on over my shoulders. The carpet on the landing and trickling down the stairs isn't very interesting, except in the way that it shows up the dirt. Beige like toast or old people, but what it does have in its favour is the way that it tickles bare feet – that delicious feeling like vanishing into a bath.

I pass through the dark hall, my toes shocked now by the cold, clean stone.

This space is unclear in the memory. Its atmosphere, its gloom has stayed with me – that much stayed like condensation on the inside of my head – but I can't see much more of it. Just the brief dark and cold and the sense of breakfast waiting at the bottom of the stairs.

SCARRING. The day upon day within which we all end up encased. The armour we make for ourselves. The damage that claims us in the end. The things that mark us as human. The things that mark us as slaves. The things that mark us as free. What we're proud of. What we hide. What we return to and run our fingers over, wondering, remembering how they happened, remembering how the beads of blood welled up. Forgetting the pain of them, turning them all into stories.

Coming into the kitchen, I hear him before I see him.

'Mind if I turn the radio on?'

That means it's going to be the news.

'No, go ahead,' Mum says.

I come to the door. The wooden table massive and unliftable right there in the middle, and Mum with her back to me, busy with the Aga making porridge for everyone, and Dad in profile, turning on the radio. There are flowers on the table, spring daffodils shining.

I am a bit frightened of my father standing in his shirtsleeves, frowning at the radio. Does part of me already know he has it in him to up sticks, to leave us? He turns and sees me and smiles, tolerant, distracted.

'Hello, darling.'

'It's quite cold down here.'

Mum turns round.

'Is it? I think you've just forgotten to put on your slippers.'

I look down at my feet, and I think perhaps Dad is looking at them too, but when I look back up at him he's studying the radio again.

'Oh, yeah. That must be it.'

I check what Mum's face looks like quickly, in case I'm going to be in trouble for only bringing my bare feet down to breakfast, but she's smiling like she thinks I'm funny, so I know I'm all right.

'I just don't know how my feet being cold can mean I have a whole cold body.'

'Maybe you've just decided that's how you feel,' Dad says, and now the radio's on and he's done his job, so he's coming over to look at me. He plants a kiss on the top of my head, and I'm staring at his tummy and the white shirt and the tie hanging down while he does. 'Morning, little one,' he says.

'Morning.'

We sit down to breakfast. Mum gives me a bowl first of all, and I put honey on it because Mum already put in raisins, so I don't have to do that bit. She gives Dad his porridge and she's got a bowl of her own, and Dad plunges the coffee, which is very different from plunging the sink. He leans across the table and I wonder whether his tie will end up in his porridge.

'All right for time?' Mum asks him.

'Yep, fine.' He sounds a bit short with her – that's a phrase I learned from Mum; she sometimes thinks that Dad is short with her, even though he's taller than she is. I don't say so, in case they've been having an argument and I go and make everything worse. But then he smiles at her, a big smile with teeth, and I can tell that they haven't been arguing, so I don't worry any more. I get my head down and concentrate on porridge.

And already I've started running out of moments to cling on to; already the scene I'm describing is ending, because we snatch our lives in jagged little handfuls of shale – we do not choose it, and some of the days we hate will last for ever, and some of the things we love will be over before they've begun, and this is one of them. This is a moment that's ending too quickly. I'm falling into a whirlpool now because on the morning in question, the porridge was too hot for me. I couldn't start it in time to keep up with the other two; I just blew on it, lifting it up with my spoon and then mixing it around.

'Are you all right, darling?'

'Yes. Just waiting for it to cool down.'

'You could add a bit of cold milk?'

'All right.'

I pour out the milk, but now it's really happening, I know I'm really losing him as the memory keeps unfurling. Because I've already let Dad get miles ahead with the breakfast, and he's sipping his coffee and he's halfway through the bowl that was filled with porridge just seconds ago, and he looks at his watch, and I can never remember these moments with the calmness they must have been filled with any more – I can only ever go back over them knowing I'm losing him, filled with panic, filled with fear. And the little girl I'm trapped in, whose eyes I'm seeing out of, is filled in turn with all my panic, my middle-aged fear, so it feels like the vessel I've poured myself into will hardly be able to take it. She'll surely have to burst like a dam and scream out what I know and she doesn't, what she never discovers in time. That this is not an ordinary day. This is the day everything terrible happens.

Dad finishes his porridge, and I've still got most of mine to eat. He pushes back his chair.

'That was delicious.'

'Do you need to get on?' Mum says. She's hurrying him away from us, she doesn't even know what she's doing, she doesn't know there's a cliff right there behind him, right where she's pushing him.

'I'd better get ready, yeah.'

'OK.'

He stands up now, and I give him a smile. No matter what face I want to make, what really happened there and then was that I smiled, and so I'm doomed to smile every time this current takes me back to this place and I live it again and see the damage.

'See you in a minute, little one,' he says, and walks away from the table. And me and Mum sit in what must, at the time, have felt like a companionable silence, finishing our breakfast. Mum has already eaten all her porridge: now she's just drinking her coffee. I get to the end of mine and I have a glass of water, and Mum asks me what I'm doing at school today, and I tell her I don't really know. Then Dad comes back into the room, and he's wearing his jacket.

'Are you on for the school run?' he says to Mum, and she nods.

'Thanks. I shouldn't be too late. Bye, darling.' He stoops again and gives me a kiss on the cheek this time. And is there anything special about it? Is it different from the thousands of kisses I've had from him before then, the millions of small, easy gestures of love parents are showing their children across the world that morning? For a long time I was convinced Dad must have been killed in an accident later that day, because I feel sure there was nothing out of the ordinary about that kiss. He was just saying goodbye to me, the kind of goodbye he said each morning when he left for work. So he must have skidded on a puddle or lost concentration, ploughed off a bridge or into a lorry, and I'd never been told about it in order to protect me from the sadness of his tearing and mangling. That used to feel to me like the only possible explanation. He didn't put his hand on my back; he didn't give my hand a squeeze. He just walked round the table and gave Mum the same kind of kiss that he'd given me, then walked out of the room, and turned one last time in the doorway.

'Love you,' he said. I like to think he was talking to both of us. Then he turned and left, and I never saw him again.

This is the memory I used to replay. I used to think the whole world might be just a series of re-enactments of this scene. I used to think it was the most important thing in the world that I re-enact it in my head as often as possible; a secret burnishing, a way of keeping all the moments bright.

SNAG. A fork in a road. A mistake. A distinctive marking.

Over the years of my childhood and adolescence, I grew increasingly uncertain that remembering that morning was what I'd been put in the world to do. First, I started to doubt whether I'd got every bit of it right. When I was a teenager, Mum told me that on the morning he left, she and Dad had a terrible row, and when I heard that I started to disbelieve the clarity of my memory.

The more closely I looked at the story as I told it, the more I wondered whether it might have changed subtly with the years in my hands, like soft clay, like oral poetry; whether I wasn't only breathing life back into what I had seen, whether I might be creating. I can't help feeling that it's pocked with inconsistencies. Now that I look once again at the words I remember my parents speaking that morning, something seems terribly wrong with them – they don't seem to have the right flavour. Did my mum ever call me 'little one'? It seems almost as if I have picked up this language from somewhere else. And where are my brother and sister in all this, why weren't they with us at breakfast? Have I scratched them out or painted over both of them, to get a clearer focus on the things I believe to be important? I should have written this memory down when it was new, before I had trailed so many times over it, confusing all the tracks.

The only detail I'm certain is real, strangely enough, is the darkness of the hallway outside the kitchen. Something in that clouded place I can't quite remember strikes a chord. There is an earthiness to the taste of that dark on my tongue. I don't know what else I'm seeing clearly, what is real and what is woven together out of fictions, out of dreams.

At school I discovered the concept of screen memories, a term coined by Freud, who suggested that people get through the firepit of life by shielding themselves from the worst of it. We construct myths, false images, shadow images that stand in place of the real events of our lives and make the traumas we've all sailed through a little more bearable. These screens, which are woven through with threads that trace back to the real life they're hiding, deflect our attention away from the things that cause serious pain by remembering. And they will make the experiences we've been through a little easier to understand; they are a way of shaping the senselessness of our experience into a story, because people need a story if they're going to understand anything. When I discovered all this, and had to confront the well-established theory that very few of the memories we carry in our head are actually real, I started to wonder what exactly it was I'd been remembering all the time I thought my way back to my dad. Had I only been telling myself a tale? Was there any more substance to the images I cherished than the gossamer fabric of a dream?

Then one day I read that scientists have shown how some memories can be erased by a person who systematically remembers a related memory. They had wired a person up to a computer, and repeatedly shown them two images in quick succession. I can't remember what the images were – let's say they were my encyclopedia and my dad. While they did this, the scientists watched which neurons fired in the brain when the person saw each of these images. After a while, a link between the two images was established, so that whenever the person saw the encyclopedia, they also thought of Dad. Whenever one set of neurons fired, the other would glow dimly as well. But then an interesting thing was observed to happen. If the person was repeatedly asked to recall just one of the two images – just the encyclopedia, say, and not Dad – the neurons that related to Dad, which fired up and showed that the encyclopedia was reminding the person of Dad, slowly faded away back into nothingness. The link disappeared once again.

So that if I were to obsessively reconstruct, say, the last time I saw my dad, I might eventually forget a lot of other memories associated with him. Every other day I'd spent with him. Every other word he'd spoken to me.

What it was possible to conclude from this, the scientists said, was that the brain discards what we don't use as often, to make room for what we seem to really need. The brain will only keep the best worn of the paths we take through our neural pathways tramped down and passable, and allow all the others to choke up with weeds. The other memories are either left walled off, little sequences of maze no one can get to any longer, or otherwise used for fertiliser, and eaten whole by the memories that take up the space they once occupied.

This shocked me. I realised I might have erased thousands of other memories of my father by obsessing over this last one, coaxing my brain into giving that morning more and more space till there was room for almost nothing else. When I tested myself, I found I remembered very little else of Dad. I wondered whether I hadn't been trying to get closer to my father after all, all those times I'd relived that precious, ambiguous morning. Perhaps I had been trying to drown him in the brilliant yellow of the daffodils on that table, so there was as little left of him in my head as possible; instead of a whole vanished childhood there might only be one image, one last thought for me to stick to the dartboard. That's how we hate things, I think – we simplify. It's easier to hate an image than it is to hate something as complex as a whole relationship between a daughter and the father who abandons his family and leaves them alone with their doubts and griefs. When we stick up a picture on the dartboard, we're covering over other things as well. Everything we make is concealing as much as it displays. Everything we say is a kind of lie, a way of hiding other things that don't get said.

When I was at school I had a friend who used to lie all the time. Hannah. She would tell the most extraordinary lies every day, and everyone knew that they couldn't be true, and I thought she must have known that, but she carried on anyway.

'I met the Pope on holiday.'

'No, you didn't.'

'I did. We went to Rome and he meets seven visitors a day and it's a ballot, and I put my name in and I got to meet him.'

'In Rome?'

'We talked for half an hour. I told him the Sistine Chapel ceiling was beautiful.'

'You're not a Catholic.'

'No. He said he hoped I'd consider joining.'

What she liked to do was make her life sound more exciting than it was.

'I've been approached by the Security Services.'

'What for?'

'They want me to help them with intelligence gathering.'

'Why would they want you?'

'Connections.'

'What connections do you have?'

'They need better connections among young people. And I know loads of spies anyway, so I could help pass on whatever they learn.'

'How do you know any spies?'

'I do.'

'Who?'

'I just know lots of spies, don't be jealous. I know one who works for an oil company in Africa. His grandfather was the head of the communist party in Europe but he was actually a British spy bringing down the communists from the inside, and his family have been working as spies ever since. And I know a spy who goes round Africa selling textbooks as cover for his secret meetings. And I know a spy who runs an art gallery in Beirut.'

'How do you know these people?'

'I just met them.'

She turned into the girl who cried wolf, of course, and after a few of these tall stories she couldn't say anything without people disbelieving her. When we were in fourth form she told me that she'd gone to see the Beatles just before they stopped playing live, and I laughed at her, I didn't believe her. It was only a few months later, when I was round at her house, that I noticed the programme for a Beatles concert in her room. She didn't mention it – it was just sticking out on her bookshelves. I asked her to show it to me and she got it down and I looked at the leaflet, and realised she might have seen the Beatles after all; I might have just assumed she was lying. I asked her what they were like to listen to when they were right there in front of you.

'It was really weird,' Hannah said. 'Because obviously there's that thing where all the girls go mad for them, Beatlemania, you know. And they just scream and fall in love all the time the band are playing. And I said to myself, I'm not going to do that, I'm here for the music, I like the songs, I'm a real fan. And then they walked on stage and everyone around me started screaming, just screaming, it was this sort of wave, and I just joined in. And I don't think I stopped till they walked off stage again. And I don't think I heard hardly any of the music.'

CURRENTS. The way that water runs after the moon. The dangers that drown us if we let them. The things that can carry us home. The patterns hidden under the surfaces that order the world we can see. Something to map. Something to plan around. Something to shock you. Something to harness and turn into power.

I turned to the facts of Dad's life to try to understand what might really have been happening on the day he left. I didn't know many of them. Until I started asking, Mum never really talked about him. But I learned that he hadn't come home from work that evening, and when Mum called a friend of his from the office she was told he'd seemed perfectly normal at the end of the day. A missing-person search started shortly afterwards. A few days later, Mum told me, she received a letter. She couldn't show it to me because she had destroyed it, but in the letter Dad had told her that he had decided he couldn't live as he was any longer; he had felt he was drowning and had to look for a different way of keeping his head above water. He promised to send money for the rest of his life, and indeed, at least for the rest of my childhood, he did.

I wish with all my heart Mum hadn't burned that letter. There must have been clues to be unravelled; it must have held secrets soft as the centres of artichokes. It might have been a trapdoor into knowing him better. But it went into the fire like so much of childhood, so much of happiness, so much of memory.

And then, years later, when I was getting ready to leave home, Mum told me that in the weeks before Dad left, he had been seeing a doctor and taking days off work. The doctor had initially diagnosed anxiety, but Dad had confided to Mum that he worried the situation was more extreme than that. And Mum had got the impression, without Dad actually saying so directly, that he wondered whether he might be on the border of schizophrenia, walking tentatively through the shallows of some real and crippling psychosis.

This revelation about my dad seemed so outlandish, so extreme and unlike anything I remembered of him, that when Mum first told me, I didn't believe her. But Mum explained to me that there'd been no formal diagnosis: it was only a feeling he seemed to have, a creeping conviction. I asked her what she meant, and she said he'd started to believe the world wasn't real. He'd started to try to live more and more in his head, in retreat from the noise of the world all around him, as a way of shutting out everything that seemed to be walling him in. He never used the word schizophrenia. It was later, when Mum talked to people about it, that she discovered the possibility of a correlation. Schizophrenia, she learned, is a kind of retreat from the world into the mind's secret compartments, a flight from reality people take when they can't cope.

If this is the whole of schizophrenia then I wonder how close any given person is to diagnosis. It seems the most human need in the world to me, the need to dive into a story. But perhaps it made it more bearable to Mum – to believe that he had been ill. So I think she clung to that, and told herself he must have been on the margins of a terrible suffering. Mum told me last of all that Dad's paternal grandfather had been committed to the Surrey County Pauper Lunatic Asylum in his forties, and his sufferings would most probably have been characterised today as schizophrenic. Somehow this made her feel able to go on, to think her husband might have belonged in such a place as well.

I went and visited what used to be the Surrey County Pauper Lunatic Asylum once. I wanted to see the place because I thought it might somehow make me feel closer to the experience of madness my mum had suspected might be taking hold of my father. I thought it might make me feel closer to him. I had tried to read about its history, but never found a book that gave much room to the people whose lives had blown them to that place. So I caught a train and went to have a look around instead.

The hospital is in London now, though London hadn't sprawled so far out when it was built, so it has the air of a secluded spot that has suffered from tidal change. Set back from Burntwood Lane, the grounds of what was now called Springfield University Hospital stretched almost the whole length of the hill that lies between Wandsworth Common and Garratt Green. There were banks of trees like clouds at the margins of the grounds that you could imagine offered shelter for half of the foxes in London. The hospital was a warren of buildings in varying states of dilapidation; some elderly and forbidding structures which had long been abandoned, some more modern Portakabins that no one had a use for any more. I walked round to the front of the building and felt I was standing in front of a Cambridge college. A large brick building, proclaiming the date of its construction as 1840 over the hospital's main entrance, set back from the road and gently embracing three sides of a square lawn, seemed to stare fixedly into the sky over my head. It was early evening, and lights were starting to glow above the lawn in the spreading dark. A hundred years ago, my great grandfather must have looked out through one of these into evenings like the one I stood in.

What I understood when I lined up the facts was that something terrible must have been roiling and burning and coming to the boil in Dad that no one knew about. Or that something unspeakably awful happened, perhaps on the way home from work that evening, that made life unbearable to him as it was.

Once I knew what I could of my dad, and saw how little that really was, I started to question how much we ever really know about the lives of others, and the minds of others, and the tides that push and pull them.

SCREENS. To be used to conceal us. To keep out the weather, the eyes of others, the shadows that hide at the edges of rooms. To keep us all safe from the fire.

Maybe it's not so strange to suspect we are all on a spectrum that ends in schizophrenia. Maybe that's what's so interesting about people – that each of us contains the seed of everything that has ever happened, and ever will happen. All of us could be anyone, if we were born into the right lives. And that's an important thing to bear in mind, for those of us who live our lifetimes out of the way – there's no more or less dignity in anybody's day.

BLANCHED. Something with all the life drained out of it. Something shocked. Something that has been saved for later. Apples in the freezer for crumbles in the later winter. A person who's heard something they don't like.

I had an appointment at Green Lanes in Devizes. After I'd seen the cat on the road I carried on driving, thinking back over all that vanished mystery. I try to keep my mind on the world as it is now, the day around me, not the world as it had been and could be no longer, but always I find that's a difficult trick.

I headed south out of Aughton through Collingbourne Kingston and Collingbourne Ducis, playing my CD of *Revolver* and singing along quietly to keep my spirits up as the barren sorrow of the Plain rolled past, and seemed to be pressing to get into the car and sit down all its sadness and its solitude beside me. I nodded as always to the church at Collingbourne Kingston, the cricket green, the old pub on the right done up in new finery.

Nothing growing in the fields now. I took the shortcut along Chick's Lane to Everleigh, and headed west through Upavon, the edges of Rushall, Chirton, Conock, Wedhampton, Lydeway, till I came to the outskirts of the town. The fields were blanched and echoing back the colour of the bloodless sky. No birds, or very few of them. Late sparrows and dun robins harrowing the soil. Here and there a crow picking its way through a hollow furrow.

Blank space, dead land. Try as I might, I can only ever feel that my life since it started has been a steady narrowing of possibility, the closing of one door after another that I never passed through. And I find it easier to dream of the future too than to live in the present, because when I think of the world after I'm gone, I imagine it as this glorious opening-out again, like the mouth of a river stretching to eat the sea – all this experience that has been caged within my small existence released from the confines of this car, this body, this bungalow and let back into the wideness of the world where anything might become of it. And that is a comforting thought to conjure with as well. So I prefer to dream of the world when it used to be wider, and the world when it will be wide again, when I am not strangling it into this small vision, even though I know it keeps my life small just to dream and not to live it.

Revolver is one of my Always discs. These are the CDs I play whenever I get the chance, as often as I can, which are with me in the car all the time, unless I take them inside to play and sing along to in the sitting room in the evenings. I made a study of my Always discs once, because for a long time I'd been aware there were certain albums I listened to more often than others, but I hadn't pinned down exactly what they were and what it was about them that I liked, I hadn't formulated any kind of system. But I like systems and I like categories and I like lists, so when a quiet afternoon opened up before me one day, I got round to making a study of my CDs and which ones really seemed to matter to me. I found the exercise comforting. Perhaps it's a way of having control, or reminding yourself of all the good things there are. What I learned when I went through all my music and identified my Always CDs was that I liked some things best partly because of the good music, but also because they belonged very particularly to an important part of my life. I suppose that's so far, so unremarkable. Music more than anything else seems to have a way of being personal to people. There are songs everyone thinks are about them, even though they can't be, and songs that people assign entirely different meanings to because of the lives they've lived. They somehow get inside us, have a way of feeling like they're speaking to us.

ALWAYS CDS. Revolver. Abbey Road. Rumours. Bare Trees. London Conversation. Sunday's Child. Solid Air. Ladies of the Canyon. Blue.

There have been times when these CDs have saved me. I have felt that I couldn't go on, then listened to one or another of them, and decided that if I just get a night's sleep, then perhaps there'll be some way forward. And there always is. There has always been a way to bear it a little longer, up until now, at least. I know that it seems silly, but it helps me, and the doctors I see, they tell me that if it helps, it helps, and I shouldn't be worried what other people think about it.

I never saw the Beatles live, but I did use to go and see John Martyn. He sang three of my Always CDs, and I loved him in the way you can afford to when you know you're never going to meet someone. He seemed to me to be bigger than life, to eat it up, to feel things deeply in a way other people couldn't. It made him a drinker, and the three times I went to hear him play he wasn't always very good. In the seventies I heard him in London and he was drunk but he could play, he could sing like an angel, and I sat in the cloud of the music and felt safe and loved like sometimes only music makes you feel. When I saw him in the eighties at a gig in Bristol, he was different; he was moody, he didn't talk to the audience during the set, and then near the end he smashed up a guitar. His voice was cracked and deeper, broken up by drink like soil cracking in the heat of summer, and he was heavier set. These were hard years on him, whisky years, and the last time I saw him, ten years ago now, he was a twenty-stone man in a wheelchair, one leg off because it became gangrenous, the alcohol almost finished with him. His voice then was only the memory of a voice, a croak that sometimes hit the tune. The man sitting next to me at the gig was enraptured, but I just found it sad.

'Isn't he amazing?' he said to me between two songs.

'Do you think so?' I asked him.

'To have kept going.'

'But wouldn't it have been amazing if he'd found a way to not hurt himself?'

'Don't you think all that experience, all that pain is what makes his voice so powerful though, makes the songs so good?'

'Do you think his voice is powerful? I think he sounds sad.'

When John Martyn died there were lots of stories about what a violent drunk he could be, how he used to beat people up, how he once beat Sid Vicious up because Sid Vicious told him he was past it. How he used to hit his wife, and struggled with heroin, and slept rough in Trafalgar Square when he first came down to London seeking fame and fortune. All the violence and the rough-edged romance of a post-war, poor boy's life, trying to find something to cling to in an unravelled country. One more churned-up kid whose family moved about and split up and whose city changed beyond recognition so he didn't have a centre any more. And then beside the stories was the music. All the reissues, all the rare live albums, all the old home videos uploaded to YouTube. This beautiful tousle-haired young man singing so deep, so full of feeling. And all these people saying that you had to have one to have the other, and I wondered whether that was really true, or whether he couldn't have lived longer if someone had set him right when he was a kid and started drinking.

The other band from among my Always CDs I've heard live is Fleetwood Mac. A few years ago I travelled up to London to the O2, and they played, and I thought they might be past it then, but once the music started I was lost. There was a second drummer behind a screen filling in all Mick Fleetwood's drumming – I could see him because I was sat so high up – but Stevie Nicks and Lindsey Buckingham still had this extraordinary thing; they still seemed to love each other. Or love the story of the two of them, I don't know. So the songs they sang together were so charged and full of feeling, and you felt you were diving back into everything you knew about them. I wondered whether it was just an act, a cynical way of revisiting who they'd once been long ago, or whether they really did love the words they sang. If that was true it must have cost them so much, night after night, all these years. But still, for everyone in the O2, they seemed electric. After the gig I walked back to Greenwich tube station and there was a boy with a guitar at the ticket machines, trying to top up his Oyster. He happened to look up at me at the same moment as I looked at him, so I smiled, to be friendly.

'Who was playing?' he asked.

'Fleetwood Mac.'

'What, the actual Fleetwood Mac?'

I parked my car at Green Lanes, and went inside to the reception desk. They know me already, so I just signed in. The NHS might well be fit for bursting, but out at the edges where there are fewer people for it to look after, you can still see how it ought to have worked. Whenever I'm in Green Lanes I'll like as not see someone else I know, waiting in a bed there, visiting a relative. And the women at reception get to know you and smile when you come in, and that's how it must have been once.

I went into the waiting room and sat down in a plastic bucket chair. There was one other person there, a young man waiting at the other end of the row: bad haircut, old tracksuit trousers and a T-shirt, tattoo of a football club crest on his right bicep. Could it have been Swindon? He glared at the floor and rocked ever so slightly, and he wasn't talking to himself, but you could see from the intensity of his staring that there was some argument inside him, waiting to get out. Many of the people who come to

Green Lanes look this way. I imagine sometimes I do. I felt calm today though, perhaps still half asleep from staying in bed too long, or maybe it was just the knowledge that snow was coming made me quiet, as if I was preparing for hibernation. I waited and rubbed my index fingers against my thumbs. I felt the roughness of my fingerprint, the softness of the flesh beneath it. This is all we can really know. Rub your thumb against your index finger – you feel the contact, you know you are alive. The rest, I think, is guesswork.

A nurse I knew came out into the waiting room, and looked at me, and smiled.

'How are you today?' she asked.

'Yes, I'm fine.'

'Are you ready to come with me?'

'Great.' I got up and followed her into the next room.

Beyond those doors, I find the world around me always vanishes, and I can never remember once I'm done with my doctor what exactly passed between us. When I try to recall those moments, what comes to my mind is the story of the seven-league boots – the man who tried to get home but couldn't, because every step he took, his boots carried him too far. If I try to put my finger on a conversation that took place in a consulting room, I find the world slipping, so that what I see instead is a day at the complaints counter refunding yoghurts, talking people out of their anger at imagined slights, imagined cruelties perpetrated against them by Budgens, which they have decided represents the smug face of some evil empire. Or I think instead of old friends I don't know any more. What I can never quite see is the room, the consultant asking me which chair I'd like to sit in, whether I'd like the window open, what's happened to me since I saw them last. The picture slides away, and I retreat into memory. And that, I suppose, is why I have to keep going to the appointments.

By the time I came back out, the light was fading. I felt unsettled as I always am by time spent with doctors, because I can never sit down with a doctor without remembering the old joke that it's the one profession with a zero per cent success rate. It always unnerves me to think that what a doctor is doing with every patient is helping them through to the day of their death, and that they probably see it all coming towards us far more clearly than we do. In Green Lanes, they don't deal very often with terminal cases. The stock-in-trade there are the worlds in our heads, and also the administering of electric shocks. Scant consolation to those who have to endure them, maybe, but the place is a centre of excellence in electroconvulsive therapy, doling out about six hundred doses a year to one poor beleaguered patient or another.

Some people are surprised to learn it still goes on, the electrocution of patients; like the application of leeches to gangrenous wounds, it's one of those things folk don't expect the NHS to still be paying out for. But it happens every day. Short-term confusion and memory loss, fugue states, almost always occur to a lesser or greater extent in the aftermath of such a treatment, but it helps people too. It does cause what you can't really get around calling brain damage – the memories lost in the shock are often irretrievable, particularly the more recent memories shaken out of place; older memories tend to have found their way home within about seven months of the treatment being administered. They roost in a different part of the brain. But the thing you have to understand about living with a serious mental illness is that it's terrible; sometimes, bad times, it's barely life at all. For the people who submit to ECT, memory loss is nothing compared to going on as they are. That's just one of those ugly, invidious truths you find people facing from time to time. The injustice of a person having to choose between electrocution and suicidal depression is repellent, but it's a choice people make six hundred times a year at Green Lanes in Devizes.

After the appointment, I didn't want to get back in the car yet, so I set off to walk into town, along the residential streets separating the hospital from the centre. As I walked, the street lamps came on and the snow started falling, and I felt the cold, but pulled my coat tighter round my neck and carried on anyway. I hoped I would clear my head a little of the clouds that had formed around me. The sky was a coal white, the colour coal goes when it's all burned away. I'm always shocked by winter, that different country we live in while we wait again for the warmth of the sun. The colours are all different, and it gets dark so very early.

The centre of Devizes always strikes me as beautiful, a lost little postcard town no one would ever think to visit. It has the feeling of being a long way from anywhere, like so many of the towns of Wiltshire. You can't walk through Trowbridge or Westbury or Calne without thinking these are places that have been forgotten, left alone.

You find that out among the villages as well, I suppose. I remember once visiting a village called Edington, a little way out of Trowbridge, because I needed to get away from myself for a night and I thought taking a tent on to the Plain and being outside would be a good way of doing it. I walked from Trowbridge until I came to this old Norman church that made me want to stop, and that was Edington. A long village with a too-busy road running all the way through it, that had grown up in the shadow of a hill with one of those white horses carved into the side. I wanted to climb the hill to try and get a good view of the Plain, because I often find I can lose myself in a beautiful view. The worms and the beetles in me go quiet and I can just look at a place.

It was getting dark when I arrived, because I'd walked a long way, and I left my bag in a ditch at the foot of the hill, trusting that no one would take it, and scrambled up a muddy gully, a deep cleft in the hillside, racing to see the moment when the sun dipped low enough over the horizon to be level with the land, and to light up every tree and hedge and divot on the Plain with its red glowing horizontal light, the magic minute at the end of the day that city people don't know happens, when the sun salutes us. In the end I was too late to catch it properly – I was still only halfway up the gully when I turned and saw that all the trees seemed to have caught fire in that late light, so I only saw a snatch of it, as much as the gully I was standing in revealed to me. By the time I got to the top of the hill and could see the whole hundred-mile view, the light was gone, and I was only looking down into the gloaming. Sometimes all we get is glimpses of things, and maybe we ought to be glad of that; maybe if we were spoiled by seeing the whole magic spectacle we wouldn't think it was as precious.

Because it was getting dark, I hurried back down the hill and went into the pub, and there I met a brickie whose surname was the same as the village we were standing in. He asked me where I'd been because he saw the mud on my boots, and I said I had climbed up the hill to try and catch the light, and he knew just what light I was meaning. He had made that climb himself, a hundred times, and told me about the different views you could take in, depending what part of the hill you climbed. He knew the secret, the magic link that sprang up between people and the land in these quiet corners.

There is one resident in this town who knows how to spot the link I'm talking about, the electrical charge between the earth and the eye that makes the whole place magical. His name is David Inshaw, and he paints the fields for miles around here, and the bodies of women, and women fully dressed in the fields and in gardens. The soft lines that make up real life. I see him sometimes, walking down the High Street. He lives somewhere in the town. I have always felt very close to him, ever since the first time that I saw his paintings, because I think he can see things in just the way I do. He can see the world as if it were a beautiful dream, a beautiful story that is happening to us, and show that dreaming back to us in paintings. He can show us how strange and secret everything is, and it makes my heart sing to know someone has found a way of telling that story about this place, this Wiltshire, this Devizes. Maybe if he had never got it down in paint, no one who had never lived here would know as clear as we do that life is a dream.

I like looking at David Inshaw paintings, because for a while I lost my feeling for the country. I could only see the other side of things, the brutal side of being there. When Fred and Rose West were in the papers, I imagined their crimes as ghosts that had crept from the Forest of Dean, and I found it so shocking, the stories that emerged, so savage and dark. I couldn't look at any country town any more and not see evil. The casual ease with which country people are able to slaughter things, the way that people are also meat, just as pigs and sheep and horses are meat. I would go into Devizes to shop and everyone I passed in the street, I wondered, what are they doing to their family? Who might they hurt this evening? For a few weeks I lost all sense of perspective. I thought maybe all the civilisation around me had been revealed to be a lie, and really everyone I met might be a child abuser, everyone was at it, everyone in their secret heart dreamed of murdering and eating other people. It was a long time before I could see the world was beautiful as well as frightening again, before I could see like David Inshaw.

When I was six years old I found a cat dead in our back garden. Rigor mortis had set in, and when I pushed one leg of it with my toe, the whole body moved away from me, as if I had been pushing a branch or a stone. I went to get my mum and she was upset, and went off down the street to find out who owned it. Knocking on doors and asking who had a ginger tom. I stayed by the cat and felt so sad for it. The body all stiff on the ground, the eyes staring.

It was strange to be thinking that evening of my father as I walked through the cold of Devizes and its air of forgetting, as the snow began falling through the early lamplight and I watched it fill the pale sky from the darkening emptiness above my head to the bright, brimming line of the horizon. Snow has a way of cocooning you while you walk through it, gathering you into your loneliness and muffling it, and I felt, as I walked, as if I had been left alone with him, with the memory of Dad, the echo of his voice. I felt almost close.

He's ended up becoming one of the few discernible themes of my lifetime, one of the organising principles of my world. The same thing happened to me again a little later. When I was in my mid-twenties, I lost my husband, too, was left to mourn him like a lost shadow, a lost limb. What I heard when that happened was an old refrain: the loss, the sense of doubt, the sense of guilt, the sense of worthlessness. I let that music take hold of me, and gave up on the big city I had moved to because it was just too bloody hard, and moved back to the place where I had started, and gave myself to remembering.

We used to like listening to music together, my husband and I. It makes the air seem alive around you, makes sex better, lifts you up out of the bodies you're both in into this other feeling. We used to go to gigs together and dance, when we both lived in London. The Smiths weren't as good as everyone says; you couldn't dance to them. We were happier when we could move our feet.

'I know I can't dance,' he used to say, 'but that isn't the point, is it. The fun's in moving – you don't have to be good.'

'It wouldn't hurt if you were a bit better, though.'

'Why?'

'Well, people look at you, and they look at me, and they think you're the sort of person I'd be seen with in public.'

'Course you would.'

'Yes, but I might want an upgrade one day if you keep on dancing like that.'

'Don't worry, my love, that's not a problem. There are no upgrades on me.'

'You're exhausting.'

He laughed. 'That's all the dancing.'

GARDEN CENTRES. What I always loved was garden centres. Ever since I was little, going to garden centres was something I used to do with Mum. There was a centre near us with a climbing frame round the back, three huge old hollowed-out trees that had been made safe and sanded down and linked together with stairs and stepladders. Mum and I would go on Saturdays, our little adventures, little escapes. We'd start in the cafe at the front of the garden centre, where Mum would have tea and I would have juice, and then we'd go round all the plants, and Mum would pick out things she wanted. I never concentrated on the names of plants when I was young, but I liked following her round and breathing in the smell of everything, loved the colours, loved helping Mum put things in the trolley and helping push the trolley along. Before we paid for everything we'd go to the climbing frame for ten minutes, which Mum called the Kickly Houses. Sometimes there'd be other kids for me to run around and play with, and sometimes there wouldn't be, but I didn't really mind either way. I was always a shy child for starters, and when it came to the Kickly Houses my favourite things were the shapes and the grain and weft of the hollowed trees, and the smell of the woodchip under my feet and the wet black soil beneath it, and the feeling of rough bark and smoothed-down exposed wood under my hands.

I have kept my love of garden centres all my life, and for as long as she was alive it was something I continued to enjoy doing with Mum. The happiest thing we shared, I think. When I visited her, more often than not we'd visit a garden centre. Usually the one that was near where she lived, where we'd sit in the cafe and talk about relations, then walk round the sale yard looking at the plants. Mum always liked to come home with something new for her garden.

'God knows why I do it – murder on the lower back, the gardening lark,' she said, though I knew she didn't mean it and was only complaining to make me roll my eyes.

'You could get one of those special low stools people have for weeding.'

'Oh yes, I've got one of those, I swear by it. Incredibly comfy. I sit there like Buddha, digging away like a child in a sandpit with the radio on.'

'*Bindweed and* Woman's Hour.'

'*Sometimes it's hard to tell one from the other.*'

She was a genius with plants. Much better than I've ever been. She somehow knew what would grow where, and what went well together; not just things that looked good side by side but those that were healthy for each other. She taught me how to grow all sorts from cuttings and from seeds, and about potting, and moving them from the greenhouse to the garden and back again in winter. All these complex processes seemed to come to her as easily as whistling a tune.

'*The starting point is very easy,*' *she liked to say to me.* '*You just have to remember they're all living things, and then you work out what they like, and what they all need to be well. Just like different people need different things, that's all there is to it. It's the same as listening, really.*' *And she was a good listener, a voracious listener, with people and with plants; she'd drink up what was said to her. So her garden was always beautiful, always alive with the promise of buds and flowers. Whenever it was dry and warm enough, she liked to be outside in it. So my visits to her would very often end up with gin in the garden.*

'*It just feels like peace out here, doesn't it,*' *she'd say to me, over the clink of ice cubes, the crackle of a bonfire, the late flare of summer sunsets, the owl's shriek.* '*It just makes sense. This is the centre of the world for me, this little square of garden. All of the rest of my life, making money and getting sleep and having something to eat, the way I see it, all that is just doing what I have to do so I can sit in this place and be happy under the apple trees.*'

By the time I reached the square with the war memorial at its centre, my hands were brittle with cold and I could feel my lip starting to shiver a little, so I decided to go into The Bear Hotel for a drink. It had been a long time since I had been in The Bear, but I used to like it there, and I needed to get warm, and I thought I could get a decaf coffee and sit by a window and watch the street. I don't know why more people don't have their coffees or teas or drinks in the bars of hotels. I hate all the cafes that have been foisted on us, all so noisy and crowded and public.

I walked through the door and found the place very familiar, decorated more or less as it had been when I'd last set foot in there. It's strange to walk into a place you've known so well, but haven't visited in a long time. I was brought up short for a moment with the thought of all that had changed, and decided, in the blurring moment of disorientation and uncertainty and regret I experienced passing through the front doors, that I would have a glass of wine after all; it wasn't too early, and I would still be able to drive after one, and I didn't feel like a coffee anyway. The bar was much the same as it had been the last time I came here. I thought of everything outside this building that had changed, all the days of the world that had been effaced, like so many pavements or byways under snowfall, and it seemed surreal to me that The Bear had remained impervious to all of it. I ordered a glass of Sauvignon Blanc, and turned around to look for somewhere near the window to sit.

QUIETNESS. A receptive state. A moment of passivity. A tensed, coiled feeling of being about to dive back into time. An alertness to the stimuli around you. A moment's sleep. A ducking out of the world. A dipping your head under the peaceful silent water.

'Who do you remind me of then?'

I looked around to see who was speaking. There was only one other person in the bar. A man of about my age, sitting at a table near the door. I hadn't noticed him when I'd come in; I'd walked straight past him. He was looking at me, the beginnings of a smile on his face, a pint on the table in front of him. It almost seemed as if he thought I might go and join him. He was a square-set man, his hair turned white, but still plenty of it. His hands were laid facing down on the table, looking hard worked, elderly, the scars laced over them of a long life spent on labour. He looked like he had never given thought to himself. He had thrown himself at life, maybe, and there had been no time for resting. What I noticed above all, though, were his eyes. Sad eyes, blue and unsettling. They hardly seemed to belong to him.

'I'm sorry?' I didn't know what else I was supposed to say.

'We don't know each other, do we though?' He looked at me seriously, forehead furrowing as if he was trying to bring a name to the tip of his tongue.

'I don't think so, I'm sorry.' I smiled in apology. The man smiled too, and shook his head, and the spell that had seemed to be gathering broke as he lifted a hand in apology.

'I'm sorry. You just remind me of someone, I think that's it. I don't know who, but there it is.'

I laughed, uncertain and nervous. After all, I didn't know who he was – he could have been anyone. And we were alone, besides the young man cleaning glasses behind the bar, his back to us. Either of us could have said anything, and no one would have known.

'I've just come in for a drink before I head home,' I told him. I didn't understand why I was still talking. Why extend the conversation any longer than was necessary? It struck me that both of us might perhaps be trying to flirt, without knowing quite what we were doing.

'Far to go, is it?'

'Not too far, no.' I felt panicky now. Every thought in my head was giving me vertigo. 'Well, I'm sorry I'm not who you thought I was.' I moved away from him decisively, walked five paces and sat down by the window at the far end of the bar. I looked out of the window at the cold street. There were no people outside save for a young woman swallowed up by the automatic doors of the Co-op. I turned my eyes to the empty sky, then looked back at the dim gleam of the spirits in their bottles behind the bar.

'I'm sorry. I didn't mean to alarm you.'

I turned to the man again. He was still looking at me, speaking up a little now, because I was further away. I wished that he'd stop. I wished that I'd never answered him the first time he spoke.

'You haven't at all,' I said.

He smiled, and finally looked away from me, looked back at his drink.

'All right. Sorry. I'll leave you to your drink then.'

I lifted my glass to my lips, and tipped it back, and gulped. It was so strange for me, to talk to a stranger like this. No one tried talking to me on an ordinary day. No one ever seemed interested. I didn't mind that. Who ever likes being talked to by strangers? Who ever goes out of their way to speak to someone they don't know, and have nothing in common with, when they don't know what they might say in response? Or is that just me? My need for control? My fear of letting go?

A silence fell on the room, and now it was there I found I regretted it. It felt odd for me and the strange man to sit apart like that, when we had just been speaking. It felt like a failure somehow. It wasn't that I had anything else to say, or even that I wanted to talk. I just felt that I would have done, if I were normal, if I really wanted to be like everyone else. An opportunity had presented itself, a chance to risk myself a little, to try to hold up one end of a conversation, and I had let it pass by. I took another sip of wine. It tasted sour, it tasted of nothing. I tried to breathe a little deeper. I was getting unsettled, and that was when I panicked, and stopped being able to take things in. I breathed in and out slowly three times, and drank more wine, and this time it tasted a little better. As long as I kept myself from getting too anxious, I was OK. As long as I kept breathing.

I turned back to where the man was sitting, staring into his beer. I wondered whether he was feeling the same regret that I did. Perhaps he, too, was preoccupied with the conversation we hadn't been able to spin into being.

I took another sip of my wine. Did it have to be that I'd failed? Did it have to be that we'd finished speaking?

'What have you been up to today?' I asked him.

He turned to look at me, surprised.

'Oh, well. That's a long story.'

'Is it?'

'Sometimes I think you can't explain the last thing you did if you don't explain everything else you've done before as well – do you know what I mean?'

'Oh, right.'

'Because how would anyone understand?' He was looking at me keenly now, his young blue eyes shining. 'How could you know what I'd done today, if you didn't know how I'd come to be there?'

I wished I'd never spoken. Perhaps he was deranged. Perhaps he was out on day release and going back to Green Lanes in the evening. One of those destitute old men who wander England, drinking, waiting to die.

'It was quite complex, then, what you were doing?'

He sighed, and shook his head.

'You don't want to hear all this. It's too long a story, and you don't know me, you don't want to listen to me banging on.'

He was right. But I was wondering now, what would someone else have thought, if they were me? What was I supposed to be thinking?

I picked up my glass, and stood, and walked over to where the man was sitting. This was how I heard the most important story of my life, the thing that decided me, the story that determined who I was in the end. I stood by the chair opposite him. He looked at me, surprised.

'You can tell me, if you like. I don't have anywhere else to be.'

I pulled out the chair and sat down.

DÉJÀ VU. When lost things come back to us. The moment when you glimpse the strings that hold you up, and hear the secret current that is drawing you on through your life. A moment's doubt that any of this ever really happened.

Two

I lost two cities, lovely ones. And, vaster,
some realms I owned, two rivers, a continent.
I miss them, but it wasn't a disaster.

Elizabeth Bishop, 'One Art'

WHEN I WAS twenty-five I was a happy man – or maybe I should say I should have been. Happy man. That must have been how I looked from a distance. I'd found a foothold in the theatre, played Horatio and Gratiano, I'd married and bought a flat with my wife, and I loved my wife, and she loved me too. It seemed like we were emerging from the chrysalis stage, having just struck out on our own, not yet knowing who we were going to be. How much the world was going to let us have for ourselves.

It does feel a little like that, being that age – like watching a caterpillar while it turns into its real self. Have you ever done that? Sat and watched him weave his cloak, or watched as the cloak twitched then broke, and a creature came out, looking different, looking new? And you didn't know what it was going to look like till it fought free and the wings emerged. Those moments are real wonders, moments I've tried to put myself in the way of. When I see a chrysalis hanging somewhere secret, I'll drop what I'm doing, watch as the little shell-like pea pod wriggles and writhes till it turns in time into a swallowtail, a wood white, a red admiral, a silver-washed fritillary. All these different dreams emerging, and you never quite know the shape they'll take till they burst out fragile, blinking in the world.

So I should have been happy but, of course, you know I wasn't. If I had been, you wouldn't be hearing this story. See, I was young and I was hungry and I didn't see how good things were. I wanted to scale the heights of my trade, and didn't care for where I was then, in the foothills. Playing the best friend or the assistant, playing the King's Head or the Half Moon. I spent my time in envy of people who seemed to have more than me, seemed to glide above me, because they'd been there longer, they'd been luckier, they were trampling me down. Osprey goshawk harrier kite.

Being twenty-five, I couldn't see this was just youth talking. All that hunger. I thought no one else in the world had ever felt the things I did. My hunger and my hunger and my hunger. So I cherished the anger that burned me, loved and burnished my rage that all the doors of the city I lived in hadn't opened the first time I knocked on them, one after another. I made sure I didn't enjoy any of the things I had around me already, because I thought that would have felt like settling for second best, like giving up. I thought if I took any pleasure in the life I had around me I would be taking my eye off the place I wanted to get to in the end. And I couldn't have told you where that was; I suppose I didn't know. I just knew it was somewhere brighter, like tree-tops after climbing, like light after shade. I had this feeling there was somewhere better. God, I must have been unpleasant. I hate myself, thinking back.

Naturally, this ambition I had in me meant I argued with my wife. I wouldn't take time off. I'd work in the evenings. I said we couldn't afford to go on holidays, because I had to work. I said I didn't have time to go out and socialise. I can see now that it was torture for her. She hadn't asked for all that time alone. All she'd done was meet a man and fall for him, and suddenly she found herself isolated in this marriage, this half-life, forever waiting for me to wake up and remember I loved her. Of course, she was ambitious for herself as well, she was young too, but I think she had perspective in a way I didn't. She found ways for herself of loving the here and now, taking things in and spending time looking hard at them, and cherishing what she found at her fingertips. It didn't seem worthwhile to her to deny herself the life she was in for the sake of one she might find in the future.

So we used to argue. Stands to reason. And one evening we had an argument that changed my life. I feel I've never got over it, even now as I sit here and tell you this story. What am I saying? I know that I never got over it. It is the centre of everything. Everything else is spread out from there, like the wreckage left after an explosion. This argument, you see, this argument knocked everything I ever did out of shape; it shook me and twisted me up and changed all that came after.

You've got to let me get to what I'm wanting to say to you – don't rush me, let me say it. I know that I sometimes talk funny, I know I don't make enough sense. You have to see, I've been through some things.

When we were young. When we were young, we never fought about anything. Or that's how it seems, thinking back to it. But the start of our love I remember as this whirlwind. Meeting in the queue of a kebab shop late one night in Stoke Newington, when kebabs still seemed exotic and strange to me. I remember the eyeshadow on her and the way she seemed to like me because she kept turning round.

'Know me from somewhere?' I asked her in the end. She just laughed and told me she thought I was some kind of creep because I was standing too close to her. But I knew that wasn't what she meant, not really. She was smiling and I liked her eyes.

'I'm just the next guy in the queue.'

'No, you're a creep who's trying to breathe in my ear.'

Both of us were a few years older than the rest of the crowd queuing for their food. We were already into our twenties, and perhaps that gave us some kind of connection. And then I suppose some bell just went off in both our heads. When she got to the front of the queue I insisted I paid for her kebab, and I got one of my own, and then she left the other girls she was out with and came and sat down with me at a table in the restaurant, one of those Formica tables with plastic chairs screwed into the ground. I remember they were red and yellow, and one of the plastic chairs cracked right through so I couldn't lean back, and I asked her where she'd been out that evening, and we agreed it was never as much fun as it was supposed to be.

'You know why no club is ever any good?' she asked me.

'Why?'

'Because men are animals.'

'And women aren't?'

'Not in the same way. It's like with lions. With lions, the females are the centre of things. In the packs, it's all about the females; they're the heart of the families. The males exist for breeding. That's all the role they have. Like a praying mantis. The females are more than that.'

'Is that all we are, all men?'

'I don't think you have to be. But I think in clubs and places like that, men choose to be. They choose to be like lions.'

'What you mean is that we behave badly.'

'Yes. Primitively.'

'But don't you think there's more to animals than that?'

'What?'

'Sometimes, you watch an animal, you end up wishing you could be more like it, I think. With no self-consciousness. Just living in the world and reacting. There's more to animals than just being primitive.'

'I suppose so.'

'People say someone's behaving like an animal and mean it's a bad thing. I don't know why people want to get away from the fact that we're animals. Of course we behave like animals. I wish we could do more of it. And only be in the moment, and not think about things.'

I remember talking to this radiant girl, this young woman who would become my wife, drunk and chatting away without any filter. God knows what I said to her that evening but I suppose I will have boasted, and made some kind of fool of myself, and over her shoulder I was interested in the kebab meat spinning slowly round. It was a novelty then. We'd both had lots of salad in our kebabs so the pittas were too big to pick up really, tomato and lettuce and raw white onion, and I had a lot of mayonnaise and I remember there was yellow mustard on the table in a squeezy bottle by the ketchup. All around us were the people of the night coming to the end of their wingspans, tired people, drunk people, all of them dressed up, all of them falling over each other. And the sound of laughter and people at their happiest, and people sinking low, all the world washing gentle like a sip of brown ale through the queue of the kebab shop Friday night. All the young people, kids who were still at school, dressed up so they looked what they thought was beautiful. I always think those teenagers out on the tiles of a Friday look so vulnerable, such fragile little things, emerging blinking, and wondering what they're going to do with these bodies they've been given. Like long-limbed foals slipping over everywhere and shying at each other.

When we were finished eating, I said I'd like to call her some time, and she said maybe I could.

'What's your number then?'

'Have you got a pen?'

'No.'

'How will you remember it?'

'I'll run home.'

'How will that help you remember it?'

'I'll get to a pen quicker.'

She laughed again. 'I've got a pen, actually.'

'Have you? Can I borrow it?'

'I don't know.'

'Why not?'

'I don't know whether you'd give it back.'

She gave me her number and she lent me her pen, and I wrote her number on my hand, and when I got home that night I was sure to write it on to a piece of paper, and the next day I called her once I was good and sober.

We liked to go to the cinema. She hated the kind of films I watched and I hated all of hers, but it didn't matter because we liked each other. The thing was the ritual, so we'd take turns going to see one of my films and one of her films, and eating popcorn, and enjoying the adverts most. We liked to go out to the pubs and drink. I don't mean heavily – she wasn't as much of a drinker as me for sure, and I've never been among the worst because I've never really been able to hold it. But we loved to go out and get a bit drunk and then take each other home. And out of little things like that came the whole of our lives. We wanted to sleep in the same bed, so we rented a flat. Four rooms in a mansion block on Cazenove Road in Stoke Newington, wooden floors, metal frames on the windows, a short walk from the place where we'd first met, over the road from where the Krays used to live. It was impossible to heat in the winter, the boiler always packed in, and everyone else living in the block was a Hasidic Jew, and never talked to us, and once a year would insist on giving us money so they could walk past our door, which was apparently part of a religious festival we never quite got our heads round.

It was a good place to live, but there weren't enough parks, as we both liked our open spaces. Only Abney Park cemetery, the winding paths through the graves and the ruined church at the heart of it, and Clissold Park beyond it, with the old house in the middle and roads all round the edges curtailing our freedom. When we could afford to buy a flat instead, we bought one. We moved south to where the parks were, and found somewhere to live at the bottom of the hill below Wandsworth Common, by a park called Garratt Green where once there had been a gypsy camp with a coconut shy passers-by would pay a penny to try their luck on.

It was always simple like that. Sometimes life can seem to flow very easy. Even getting married was simple. We'd been out and it was late, and we were walking along the towpath of a London canal, arm in arm, singing songs to each other. And she stopped and looked into the water.

'Who would you want to get the call first tonight if you fell in?' I asked her. She looked at me, quizzical. I didn't know quite what I'd said.

'Are you going to push me in?' she asked.

'No. I just wondered who you'd want to hear first, if you got into trouble.'

She thought about this for a moment.

'Well, you, I suppose,' she said. Then she took my arm again and swayed away from the water and we carried on walking.

I thought about what this meant while the moon's reflection chased us along in the water like a dog loping at our side.

'You know what that means, don't you,' I said after a while, as we paused for a second to read the graffiti on an old factory with the windows all stoved in.

'What's that?' she asked, and I turned and she was looking at me.

'Well, surely if we're the ones who'd hear first then we ought to be married, I think?' Maybe it wasn't as romantic as it should have been, not traditional like you're supposed to do it. But it felt real at the time, in the shadow of the caved-in factory, standing above the deep shimmer of the dull canal. Everything was always simple like that, until the fight that ended everything.

It was one of those fights about nothing. Every argument is about nothing and everything, you know? It was one of those fights about nothing. The dry wood builds up underneath you both, and then a little spark, a little tinder. I think you never see the whole of a fight between two people, because it's not the words exchanged that matter, it's what goes unspoken. We were having one of those fights. I think it started because I'd said I wouldn't be home in time the next day for dinner, I think that was all we really argued about. The dry wood builds up underneath. I've played the conversation back so many times, I don't really know any more what's true and what parts of that old movie I might have invented. To make myself look better or make myself look worse, depending on the mood I'm in when I set to remembering. The thing about memories, I tend to find, is the wind has a way of changing every time you visit them, like those gnarled haunted trees you find on the wild coasts of Cornwall.

I think those twisted trees that overlook the oceans of the world all look like fires as well, frozen moments in the life and death of a fire you can tell must have twisted and raged and hurt so much, just from the one still memory of it caught in the tree. I think those trees look just like arguments. Frozen fires. One small instance of a fire that is raging somewhere still, in the heart of the tree in front of you, maybe. A glimpse of some glorious greater violence.

'Why not?' She was sitting on the sofa in the living room, looking up from a book, half hurt, half angry. This was the start of the fight and the rest of my life, my half-life. That's why I'm telling you what she said to me.

'A meeting moved later. It's turned into drinks so I think it'll be easiest if you don't wait for me. Then I won't feel like I'm keeping you hungry.'

'Well, as long as you don't feel guilty.'

I used to get so frustrated when we talked like this, how she couldn't see that all the work I did was done to try and make our lives better. It seemed so unjust that she became hostile just because I was busy. All of it was supposed to build us up, after all.

I knew men who went home to their partners and told the same stories I did, but told them as lies, because in fact they were off in the evenings with other women. Why couldn't she be happy that I wasn't like that? Why should I have to apologise for fighting to make our lives better? Was it just as unfaithful to leave her alone for the right reasons as the wrong ones, the liars' reasons? I couldn't believe they counted the same. But then, what is marriage if it isn't a promise to be together? So however you miss those nights, haven't you betrayed something? Perhaps it hurts the same not to be wanted, not to be needed, whatever the reason.

I didn't think all this at the time. This has all come to me in the decades since my wife and I were parted.

'Don't be like that.'

'Like what?'

'I can't help it if I have to work, can I?'

'Apparently not. Apparently you never can.'

'I don't think this is fair.'

It went on like this. You don't need to know every little detail – you've had these arguments yourself a thousand times, I'm sure. You know how they go. As they unfold, you both get hurtful, you both get cunning, find little ways of taking the high ground away from one another. We went the same way as all those other rows around the world do, bringing up little slights we hadn't mentioned at the time, using words like 'always' and 'never', turning things into absolutes that had only just crossed our minds, no more permanent than the wind, letting things get bigger as they echoed between us. And then I remember my wife throwing out a barb that really stung me, and then I couldn't be in the conversation any more.

'If you only really love yourself then why did you fucking marry me?'

It hurt me in a way the rest of our bickering hadn't done. It left a different mark, you see. She caught my eye when she said it, and for a moment the whole charade we were performing seemed very small and worthless, because I think we both knew she was telling the truth. We looked away from each other very quickly, as if we had both been scalded, but there was no denying what we had seen. It was real as the sun through clouds, the sun breaking over treetops in the morning.

The thing was that I only really loved myself. The moment she said it I knew she was right. I only really loved myself. That hurt. It hurt, as well, to fear as I looked in her eyes that she had known this much longer than I had, and she had put up with it, she'd married me all the same. I couldn't understand it, couldn't understand how she could be happy with that. She deserved better, didn't she? How could she have thought I was enough for her to settle for, knowing as she did that I wouldn't ever quite put her first? I felt ashamed thinking of the compromise she had accepted.

I didn't know how to react to this new discovery we'd made. Sometimes couples happen on truths like these, like little shards of glass that shoot from the sideboard while you sweep away bread-crumbs into the tips of your fingers, blades that slip into your palm while you wash up. I remember I looked at her. I became quiet and still. I wondered what I was supposed to say.

'Don't say that.'

'Is that a bit close for comfort? Sorry.' She stared at me again now, defiant, recovering herself. It had been said. She would have to see it through now. She seemed suddenly very powerful to me then. It made her very powerful to look at me as if she was saying, I knew this about us all along. I knew this about us, and I accepted it, and I've lived with it, and you didn't even know it was happening. I've been sheltering you from yourself all the days we've spent here under this roof, and you never knew it. Her look made me feel very small. I wanted to get away from this feeling, this frightening new knowledge of myself I'd found among the barbs my wife had spread on the ground for me. I wanted to run and hide and be on my own and try to understand what it meant, what I'd felt pass between us, this honesty, this heartbreaking honesty. Some people are fight and some people are flight. I've always been the second one. Like deer you meet in a wood, I'll start away, I'll watch from a distance that feels like safety, then I'll turn tail if someone gets any closer.

'I don't want to talk to you if you're going to be like this.' I was surprised because she laughed then. I saw she knew how strong she was as well as I did.

'What a surprise.'

'What do you mean?'

'Always running away.'

'That's not fair.'

'Is that not what you're doing?' She leaned forward on the sofa. I can still see her now, my beautiful wife, her hair falling over her shoulder, the light catching the left side of her face, eyes sparkling. My beautiful wife. 'In your dream life you'd find a place to hide where no one could ever find you. You'd find a way never to have to face up to anything.'

I turned around and picked up my coat.

'I'm going for a walk.'

My wife leaned back on the sofa again, and sighed, and shook her head. I recall, thinking back to that moment now, that she was magnificent. Like some magical creature, a goddess, something ancient, something more real than the rest of the world. At the time I couldn't see it. I was angry. I just wanted to be away from the light in her, wanted to be on my own.

'Of course you are.'

'We'll talk later. I don't want to talk to you now when you're just being cruel.'

'And it's me who's cruel, and it's you who's just walking out on us again, is it? You're just going to change the scene, but I'm the bad guy.'

I looked at her one last time before the water closed over.

'We'll talk later.'

Then I turned around and walked out of the flat. And here's the thing. In all the years I've lived through since, I've never seen my wife again.

As I remember, it had started to rain, so I pulled my coat close round me, and put my head down, and started to walk. I didn't know that was going to happen. I didn't have any idea where I wanted to go. I just felt angry; I'd felt caged in the room I was in. Time to throw off the cobwebs, time to pace and eat the world like the tiger, devouring one landscape after another, stride and stride and stride, bewildering everything underfoot. I set off. I just wanted to get away from my wife and our argument, find a breath of silence before I had to go back to our home in an hour or so, and go through the process of making up with her again.

So I walked up the hill by our house – we lived at the bottom of a slope that took quarter of an hour to walk, and landed you in a very different kind of London when you got to the end, a much more elegant London than we could afford. I walked up the hill quickly enough to get out of breath, because I felt angry, and that's part of the way we work off anger, isn't it; through the body, through the lungs. It is like poison we drain, blood to be leached out. I didn't look around me as I went. It was raining; that was all I needed to see, the water falling round me, gradually heavier, louder, drumming on the ground, till I walked at last in a downpour, and my hair was soaked and plastered to my head. I came to the park at the top of the hill and decided to step out of the weather for a little while. I didn't want to go home again just yet and carry on the argument, and I felt cold and wet through, and thought a drink might make me better.

So I went into the pub on the corner of the common, and ordered a pint, and I sat down and drank it. I didn't think about much while I sat there. I let the energy in me die down, turn gradually into emptiness, and sat and watched my glass as it emptied also. The bubbles climbing up the side, the dull glow of the pub lights through the liquid. The tidal markings of the foam in rings on the glass as it receded into nothingness again. I let the feeling drain out of me, and listened to the people talking at the tables nearby, my eye caught every now and then by the girl serving drinks behind the bar. I remember she seemed happy to be doing her work, seemed to enjoy herself polishing the glasses, and it struck me as strange, to see someone happy like that. Like I already told you, happiness was a state I tried to keep away from. I thought it was a way of blunting the knife, and I needed to be sharp, I needed to cut through the world till I got to the centre. But as I sat there, drenched and cold and low and unable to string two thoughts together because I was tired – I'd exhausted myself with a week's tension and the walk up the hill and the heat of the argument – I remember envying the girl behind the bar. She watched the image of the lights above her head gleaming in the glass, and smiled, and put it back on the shelf, then started on another, and made it look like there was nothing else in the whole world that could ever matter except that work.

Watching the lights in the glass and the girl concentrating on the cleaning drew me reeling into the memory of a holiday I'd taken with my wife. She'd been ill during the summer, and we'd gone away to Snowdonia to climb the mountain and stay for a few days in Betws-y-Coed. Snowdonia was dreadful – she found it difficult, not having fully recovered from her illness, and I was amazed by the boredom and monotony of it, as the views gave way to cloud and damp and persistent rain. When we got to the top we could see nothing; the last few steps to stand at the summit were almost too slippery to take, but we took them, then turned and walked back down.

Things were happier in Betws-y-Coed. Over the river from where we were staying was a stretch of riverbank where herons would pick their way through the water, and oak trees and beech trees shadowed the grass, and we spent one afternoon of almost impossible happiness lying there on the grass beside one another, half awake and half asleep.

'All your senses work differently around trees, don't they,' she said.

'What do you mean?'

'Look up.' I looked up, into the branches of the oak tree watching over us, into the leaves and the dappling light.

'Yeah?'

'You don't see in the same way. You see layers and layers of light, like you're not looking at one thing, but hundreds. Not one world but hundreds of worlds intersecting.' She propped herself up on her elbow to look at me, warming to her theme. 'And you hear things differently around trees as well. The rain is like applause in trees. The wind is like the sea. It's like they're doors into different places.'

'I had an idea for a story once, where all the memorial arches of the First World War were doors into different planets, and soldiers could cross a hundred years just by walking through them, and walk out of the past, or walk back into the trenches.'

'That's what I think trees can do as well. Like trapdoors,' she said. Then she lay back down again. 'Look at that, up there. It feels so good, the way the sun comes down through the branches and I can see layer on layer of light. I can feel my eyes are so much more relaxed than when I look at an open field. Why is that, do you think? What's the difference? Why does this feel so calming?'

I tried to come up with something to say in reply, but found no answer. I lay with my arm around her and we watched the branches breathing gently in the almost indiscernible breeze over our heads, lost and silent and happy on our backs in the oak shade on the bank of a shallow heron river in Wales.

After a while I calmed down, and I started to feel sorry for the way I'd walked out. I thought about the meeting that was going to keep me and my wife apart the next day, and wondered whether it really mattered. I hadn't tried to protect the time we had together; I hadn't thought about her, I'd just moved things about in my diary. I'm not proud of it, but that was the person I used to be. I wondered whether it wasn't a little unfair of me, to come in and tell her she'd be eating on her own the next day. Perhaps she deserved better than that. When I got to the end of my pint, I decided I didn't need another one. I would head back out into the rain, and down the hill, and let myself back into my home, and I'd apologise. It would be the best thing to do. Sometimes it frustrated me that I had to spend time away from work, away from ambition; but that was life, and I had to learn how to live it.

It's the great challenge we all go through in our twenties, isn't it? Finding a way to fit ourselves, the endless possibilities we have within ourselves, into the river rushing round us. What you had to learn to do was slow down just a little bit, let life happen to you every now and then, not try and be always rushing headlong into it.

So I left my empty glass on the table, and stood to put my coat back on, and called thanks to the girl behind the bar, and turned and walked out of the pub to start for home. And that was when the trouble started.

I opened the door of the pub and stepped out, and was met at once by the curious feeling of having become lost. Do you know the feeling I mean? Sometimes you'll wake, and you'll have it in the middle of the night. In your gut. You don't recognise the room you're sleeping in – you can only remember the outlines and confines of some childhood bedroom; the rest of the world you've lived in since then has somehow faded away. It's terrible. The world turns black and you don't feel as if you have the strength to deal with it. That was how I felt as the door of the pub closed behind me.

I looked around, trying to understand why I was feeling like I was, and that was when I started to feel a sense of panic, a dreamlike sense that something unreal was happening to me. I noticed that it had stopped raining. It seemed to me I wasn't looking out at the common near my flat any more. It seemed as if I was standing in the middle of a wood, surrounded and drowned in the dark of a thousand tall, silent evergreen trees. I breathed in, and the scent in the air was of dry pine needles, the burning cinnamon flavour of dry woodland, as if it hadn't rained there in for ever. I filled my lungs, and felt I was drawing the hearts and scents of spruces and larches and bog myrtle into my body. The rich, smoke voices of those different trees were mingling in me, and I knew I was far from civilisation. I looked up, fifty feet up to the canopy of pine trees looming over my head, and it didn't even seem like it was evening any more. It looked for all the world as if the sun was about to rise, as if I had walked out into early morning. And the trees whose breath was filling my lungs seemed for a moment to be speaking to me – they breathed their secrets round my ears; I heard them tell me, *You have not emerged just yet. You are not your real self.* And the image came to me unbidden of the way fire throws shapes over a wall as it burns up, flickers out different lives in its embers, faces and creatures like the shapes in clouds, budding then burning.

I thought I must be hallucinating; or perhaps I was having a stroke. Or was I falling into some different kind of sickness? Perhaps I was losing my sight. Perhaps my brain couldn't understand my eyesight was going, and had started remembering scraps of images, old memories I didn't know I'd lost, and trying to make sense of them, trying to make them look like something I knew. I blinked, rubbed my eyes. The wood was still around me. I waited for pain to come, thinking of the stroke, but none came. No stabbing pain in my arm, in the back of the brain. I reached out my hands and flexed them, and found that I could see them in front of me. And yet there was something strange about them, something uncanny that I couldn't find the words for. As if everything around me was fractured and no longer familiar, as if everything was far away. I turned round to look back at the pub and it wasn't there.

That was when I felt really afraid. Behind me, the forest stretched away tree upon tree until it became deep blue darkness, wild and indistinct. I saw no life there, though I imagined the creatures that must be picking through it: the rats and mice, the grass snakes and adders, the blackbirds and weasels and badgers and hedgehogs, pine martens, polecats and stoats. The vision of a pine marten snaking through the branches overhead made me shiver as I cast about, looking for the door I had just walked through. And the smell of the pine needles was like heat round me, and looking up at the roof of the forest once again, I thought I saw stars overhead.

Not a stroke then. Something stranger was happening. I realised I must be in some kind of dream, either because I was hallucinating, or because I had passed out for some reason as I left the pub, and was now experiencing a very vivid imagining as I lay there on the pavement in the rain, waiting to be saved, waiting to be lifted up and slapped awake by some passer-by. It occurred to me then that this felt like stepping into a movie. It felt nothing like the dreams you have on an ordinary night. It was much crisper and clearer than those, almost as if it were life itself.

For a moment I stood still and almost persuaded myself that I was simply dreaming. I didn't dream very often, much less than some of the women I've slept beside over the years, who would be able to tell me the details of their dreams over coffee almost every morning. My wife was like that; she would brim-fill with dreams each night, and some trace of them always seemed to cling to her the next day; she could always recount part of them. Sometimes she spoke to me, whispered things or tried to wake me to keep me safe, all the time dreaming. There were different worlds within her that she visited at night. That was rarely the case for me. If I did dream, I hardly ever remembered. Sometimes when I woke, the dim image of some dance I'd been poured through would echo back to me for a little while. Something I'd read in the paper and played out at night in the fields of my imagination. Something from work that had followed me into sleep. But most of the time I woke and felt as if I hadn't dreamed at all. So perhaps this kind of dream I'd fallen into seemed strange to me simply because it was something I hadn't experienced yet – a dream that felt the same as waking. Perhaps my wife experienced this all the time, and this was why she always remembered what she dreamed.

I turned a complete circle there in the forest, checking to be sure I hadn't somehow missed the pub, and wasn't still standing on the common where I thought I ought to be. If I could have just gone back inside, that would have been simplest of all. But the pub wasn't there any more. I thought of calling out, but something seemed to stop me. What if there was someone else out there in the dark? What if there was someone hiding? Once that thought had crossed my mind, I felt a little colder and wanted to get away. So for want of anything else I could think to do, and because there was a chill in the dawn air that had started to take hold of me, I began to make my way across the soft carpet of pine needles stretching out ahead underfoot, waiting for the moment when the dream ended and I woke up. Above me, the sky seemed to be lightening on my left. I guessed that must be east and walked towards it.

I hadn't been walking long before I realised this couldn't just be a hallucination. The silence of the forest, the scent of the pine needles was too real, the softness of the needles underfoot, and I could really feel my muscles working as I walked. It crossed my mind that perhaps I had lost some time – perhaps I was in a real forest, on a real morning, watching the light flood the sky above my head, and the piece of the puzzle I was missing was eight or nine hours between this moment and the moment when I had stepped out of the pub. Amnesia; or I'd hit my head; or sleep-walking; or perhaps I'd even been abducted. That would make a kind of sense. But I didn't have a headache, or any bruises I could feel, or anything like that. Could I have been sleepwalking all night, and woken up here?

What was certain was that the forest was real. I walked all through the dim daybreak, and saw the pale colour of the trees awaken, and heard the birdsong echoing through the branches in greeting to the sun. I made out a few of them, a dizzying variety. The calls of the pheasant, the nightjar, the tawny owl, the wryneck and the dove. I started to get thirsty, and I felt hungry, and I didn't know what I was going to do.

My first concern was for my wife. The thought that she was still at home alone and waiting for me, and that I was out here, not knowing how far I'd travelled away from her, made my chest tight with fear. I couldn't imagine what she would be thinking, if it really was the case that a whole night had somehow passed without me noticing. Would she have slept at all? Perhaps she would have assumed I'd got drunk in some pub and gone home with someone. Perhaps right now she was deciding this was the end for us. Or maybe she would have guessed the other way, and ended up calling the police instead, and even now someone was planning a search for me.

It was at this moment that I noticed the dirt under my finger-nails. Dirt worked into the pores of my hands, as if I'd been gardening for days on end. For the first time since I'd found myself in the wood, I looked down at my body, made a quick check of what I was wearing, what state I was in. The knees of my jeans were covered in mud. My boots were caked in it. There were salt marks on my shirt where I must have been sweating. And none of my clothes were my own. I looked at my hands again, and I couldn't be certain, but I felt as if they were somehow different. Finer, more elegant fingers than my own. And yet it couldn't be possible. I was experiencing some kind of weird estrangement from my own body, like the people who try to saw off limbs on LSD. And didn't my whole frame feel different, now I thought about it? My shoulders narrower, my body hollower at the waist?

Something was terribly wrong. I was wearing someone else's clothes, lost in a place I'd never seen before, and the more I thought about it, the more I felt certain I hadn't just blacked out and lost a night. I didn't feel tired enough for that to have happened. I didn't feel groggy or drugged. I was sure I hadn't been asleep. It felt like fifteen minutes after I'd walked out of the pub on to the common near my home.

Desperate for help, I started to shake because I felt weak, I felt afraid. Through the trees, I saw something I hadn't noticed before. Glimpsed dimly in the wood's dark, almost concealed by the serried ranks of pines standing around me, I saw the gleam of a vehicle parked up in the wood. I didn't know how I hadn't noticed it sooner. I hurried towards the vehicle. As I came closer I saw it was a taxi. Not a black cab, but a car with a sign in its window marking it out as a licensed vehicle. It had been parked at the very end of a mud track in the forest's near-dark, and its owner was nowhere to be seen. I strained my eyes looking for a movement, a face, a body coming into view. I filled my lungs once more and shouted at the top of my voice.

'Hello?'

I listened to the scattering, ricochet echo of my call from tree to tree, skittering like a squirrel, like a bird in autumn leaves. The strange thing in a wood like that one is that your voice doesn't echo as you'd imagine it would. Your voice drains into the trees as if they were starving. It's a clear, crisp, feeble sound, to hear your own voice calling in a place like that. A sound to remind you that any moment now the world is going to forget you; it will swallow you up like trees swallow voices, and you're fooling yourself if you ever thought otherwise.

'Help!'

I listened again. Again, nothing.

Then a thought occurred to me. I reached into the right-hand pocket of my jeans, and found a car key there. I tried it in the lock of the car, and the car opened for me. I looked inside. Nothing.

Just an empty vehicle, and the sense of something waiting. What was it? What was it that was waiting for me?

Could the man whose clothes I was wearing, whose car I was standing beside, still be out there in the woods somewhere, lost among the trees? Was it possible I'd stolen the clothes he was wearing and then somehow forgotten what had happened, and now he was out there in need of help? I peered into the wood. It seemed to go on for ever. It was a miracle I'd found the car. As if I had been guided. As if something bigger than me had known the way, and brought us here together, the car and me. But would I know to find it a second time?

'Anyone out there?'

I listened again. There was nothing. Only the distant cries of birds. I had no chance of finding anything out there. If they weren't going to come to me, there was only one thing for it.

I got in the car and shut myself inside. Nothing in the back seats. Just wipe-down leather seat covers and the sickly smell of air freshener. The silence in the car had a different quality to the silence of the forest. Here, I knew I was alone. If there had been another soul inside this box with me then I'd have heard the breathing.

I shivered, and locked the car doors, then quickly checked in the footwell of the back seats, because sometimes that was where killers hid in films. And then they sit up on the back seat behind you with piano wire as you drive along. Of course, there was no one there. I was being paranoid. I wondered whether I should check the boot, but something about that thought made me afraid, made me begin to sweat, so I started the car instead, gave up on the thought of whatever was out there in the woods, and drove off in search of a tarmac road. I had to get back to my wife as quickly as possible. That was all that mattered to me now. I had to get home and work out what had happened, because something had somehow gone terribly wrong and I couldn't get my head round it.

When we are under pressure, our minds race at once to the darkest places. We assume the most terrible things are happening. The woman you love might have died. There might be a killer in the boot of your car. There might be a killer in the woods. The same is true when we pass through dark places. Confronted with a shadow, or a door we've never seen beyond, the mind plays tricks as well, and shows you horrors.

After a minute's bumping along the overgrown tractor track, I reached a road. It ran from north to south, as far as I could tell from the position of the sun, which was bleeding its light now into the early sky, and I didn't know which direction I should head in. My only priority was to get home. From there, I could deal with whatever had happened. All that mattered was getting back to my flat. Down the road I saw a battered road sign. It seemed that I was on the edge of the Savernake Forest, if the words on the sign were to be trusted. I couldn't understand how I had got there. But I didn't care now. It hardly mattered what had happened, not for the time being. I just needed to get away from where I was. I drove on to the road and headed into the morning, hands wrapped tight around the steering wheel, eyes staring, shoulders hunched with tension.

In the years since, I've read a deal about the Savernake Forest. Because it's where my trouble started, I connect it always with the way things went wrong. It is a private forest, the only one in England, and in its great days stretched from Inkpen to East Kennett and all the way to the Collingbournes. As the centuries passed, the forest started to shrink: little by little it was turned into field to be ploughed. Because the forest has never been sold it has been well protected, better indeed than any other forest in Europe, so there are many ancient trees grouped together there in a way you don't find anywhere else. They all have their beautiful names – Big Belly Oak, King of Limbs, Duke's Vaunt, Spider Oak, Amity Oak.

In other corners of Europe, people would flock to these trees. They would be the *Tanzlinden*, the dancing trees, centres around which societies whirled as they had done for centuries past. In some places, people even dance in the trees, building ladders and platforms and stairways to take you up into the branches, take you into the air as if you were climbing the Faraway Tree. In Kasendorf there are still dancing trees like these. In England, these trees seem to hold less fascination. They are hidden in the woods and people drive past them; people never see them, people never stop.

I drove for ten minutes through the waking day, unable to come up with any answers to explain my situation. Nothing I had touched since I walked out of the pub made a moment of sense. So I let the road roll under me like water down a windscreen and tried not to panic, just tried to keep my eyes on the road, one white line passing after another.

I saw a sign coming up for a service station, and slowed down. I could use the bathroom, get some water, get something to eat. I pulled off the road and parked by a petrol station with a cafe inside, the car pointing uphill so that as I turned off the engine I had a view of a stubbled field and a vast, cloud-scudded sky above the brown earth, the clouds slowly wheeling across my field of vision in a pale and slicing wind. I got out of the car, noting as I did the mud caked along its sides, then locked the doors and hurried across the empty car park to escape the bite of the wind. It was one of those run-down, hilltop Little

Chef places, paint peeling, one or two staff moving soporific-
ally within, cracks in the car park tarmac, ketchup congealing
in the dispensers on the tables. I can't help but love these places.
They belong to another time, and who can resist the nostalgia
of everything vanished? I reached the door of the cafe and
opened it, and walked in.

But what I saw when I walked through the doorway wasn't the
run-down cafe I had expected. Instead, I was standing in some
kind of caravan, the light of a rain-drenched afternoon washing
out the colours all around me, a straggly-haired, beaten-down-
looking woman of about thirty sitting on one of two single beds
in front of me, holding what looked like a funeral urn in her
hands. I looked down at my own hands and found that I was
holding an urn as well. And I saw my clothes had changed. We
were both wearing cheap raincoats of dull green. I looked at
the woman on the bed, and she looked back at me. She wasn't
alarmed to see me, didn't even seem surprised. Her pale face, with
its dark rings like wells around her eyes, seemed lit for a moment
by a kind of compassion at seeing me come into the room, as if
she was glad I was there. As if she knew me. I held on tightly to
the urn in its coldness.

'There she is then,' the woman on the bed said.

Who was it I was holding? Who had it been? I didn't want to
be here, standing in some stranger's static caravan, holding the
remains of some woman I didn't know. This couldn't possibly be
happening, it was absurd. I wouldn't accept it, wouldn't tolerate
this, it was too much, it was madness. I turned around and opened
the door of the caravan behind me. The woman sitting on the bed
made no sound. I saw a chest of drawers to the right of the door,
and placed the urn in my hands on top of it, then turned back to
face the woman.

'I'm sorry,' I said. She didn't reply. She just stared at me blankly. I walked out of the caravan and shut the door behind me. Then I looked over to my right, to where I'd parked my car. But then my legs seemed to give way beneath me and I sank to the ground, and my hands went up to my temples and I pressed the heels of my palms against my head. I could feel I was shaking, I could feel my mouth was hanging open, because I couldn't cope with what was happening to me. The car wasn't there any more. I wasn't in the car park. Somehow, I hadn't even stepped back outside. Instead I was in some kind of tunnel. Against my back I felt cold metal. I looked behind me and saw I was leaning against a large metal door painted rustproof grey, a huge heavy door that looked strong enough to withstand an explosion. I swivelled round and placed my hand against it, felt the shock of the cold steel. I closed my eyes where I sat, shut them very tightly, as if I were a child trying to wish away a nightmare. I opened them again, and the door was still in front of me.

For a minute I didn't move at all. I didn't dare turn and look at the tunnel behind me. I didn't feel strong enough to stand up and try the door. I needed to be still for a moment. I was very scared now, convinced I was in terrible trouble. I needed to work out what was happening to me.

It seemed as though every time I closed a door behind me, I entered into a different world. It was a ludicrous thought to contemplate, and I felt mad even phrasing it, but there it was all the same – that was what seemed to be happening to me. I'd walked out of the pub, and into a forest. I'd walked into the cafe, and found myself in a caravan, dressed in someone else's clothes, holding an urn. I'd fled the caravan, and now here I was sitting in some kind of tunnel, hand against cold metal in the concrete dark.

I still couldn't convince myself I was dreaming. Things felt too real, the edges too sharp. The sweat I could feel on my skin was real sweat; the thirst growing in my throat was really happening. So there must be some other explanation. This must be some kind of psychotic episode I was trapped in.

I tried to calm my breathing and slow my heart rate down. I stayed very still and tried to take control of myself. What I wanted to do, I thought, was wait for all this to stop happening. It was some kind of malfunction in my brain, and I just needed to let time pass while my mind recovered its lost balance. There was no need to be frightened; that would only make things worse. These scenes I was seeing were some kind of illusion, and if I stayed calm, they would fade, I felt certain. They had to. They would fade.

The pounding in my chest eased a little as I forced myself to breathe in through my nose, out through my mouth, in through my nose, out through my mouth. Like they taught us when we started out in acting. I opened my eyes and saw the huge metal door in front of me. It was set into a concrete wall. I followed the line of the wall with my eyes and turned to look down into the tunnel. It was about ten feet wide and ten feet high, a large space, stretching away for about thirty feet to another doorway, opening into a larger space still, which seemed to be filled with bright lights and plants. Halfway down the tunnel I was in, to my left, was a second open doorway through which I could see a little natural light streaming in. It fell in pale bars across the bare concrete floor of the tunnel, lapping almost as far as the right-hand wall: a set of faint gold tiger-stripes on the floor. I got up from where I had been crouching and went towards the daylight, into the small side room.

The daylight was coming in through a window high up near the ceiling of the room, which had bars covering it and frosted glass in place, which meant I couldn't see through to the world outside. The window was too high for me to reach up and take a closer look, and there was no furniture in the room for me to stand on. It occurred to me for the first time that I might be trapped in this underground bunker, if that was what it was – I might not be able to leave as easily as I had the caravan, or even the forest. If there had been a door I could close and open, I could have tried out the trick that I seemed somehow to have learned, shut it behind me and got away from here, but the doorways I had seen so far were open apertures. So I would have to find a way out of wherever I was by myself this time.

I looked away from the window and examined the little room I was in. On the floor lay a sleeping mat, like the ground mat I used to take camping when I was in Scouts, and an old, battered-looking feather pillow. No sleeping bag, no mattress – whoever had been living here had been making do with very little. On the other side of the room from this rudimentary bed was a small electric stove, plugged into a power cable that snaked away out of the room and on down the hall I had just left behind me. The stove had two hobs, and needed cleaning. Either side of it were a pile of bowls and a saucepan, and a stack of what looked like a hundred packets of instant noodles. Stuck to the wall with Scotch tape above the electric stove, about three feet up the wall, was a calendar, decorated like something you'd see in a Chinese take-away, all dragons and lanterns entwined round the list of months, which was written in English. A hundred packets of instant noodles. Clearly, someone was sleeping and eating and living here. They had made this concrete room with its high window into a shelter from the world, and gathered together enough to keep them alive. I wondered where the water was, the sink, the toilet. Those must be further on into the bunker, if they existed at all. I hoped with sudden pragmatism that they did.

It occurred to me that it was absurd, to be able to think so practically about drinking water and toilet facilities, when I should have still been focused above all on my wife, who I had left behind only a little more than a few hours ago. I should have been focused on trying to get home. But so much was happening so quickly. I felt like I was leaving that kind of logical thinking behind, because those concerns, no matter how much they mattered to me, simply were not as urgent as what was in front of me right here, right now. I was lost enough that I only had room to think about what I could see immediately before me. The rest would have to be sorted out later.

My clothes had changed again. And my body felt light, as if there was almost nothing to me, and once again, when I looked at my hands, again they seemed different, as if there was something wrong with them, though I could not find the words for what it was. Some blockage in my brain held back the answer, so that I just stared at my hands and could not understand them, these delicate objects that did not seem to belong to me. I couldn't help noticing that all this shocked and panicked me a little less this time – already, the survival instinct was kicking in; I was becoming accustomed to this new pattern to my life. This was the fourth set of clothes I'd found on my body since I stormed out of my flat, and I hadn't changed into or out of any of them, but already that had stopped surprising me. My attention had been claimed by other things.

Was it possible that I was stepping in and out of different lives? I thought of the story of the man with the seven-league boots, who kept missing home, overshooting and finding himself in a

different wilderness with every step. Was that me? Was that what had happened?

I left the room with the bedroll and the noodles and the window, and walked further on down the hallway into the bunker's main chamber. I came to the end of the entrance tunnel and saw a room open up before me, stretching back at least a hundred feet to where I could see another, similar space opening up. In both of the rooms were row upon row of plants, growing up almost to the same height I was, organised under serried ranks of blue strip lights that had been rigged to hang a little above head height, all the way to the back of the room. They flooded the room with blue light and gave it a sickly, alien look that was accompanied by an intoxicating thick sweet scent coming off the plants. I could feel the heat of all that electricity burning in front of me. I stepped towards the first row of plants, and examined the leaves and the buds at the tips of each stem. Some had started to flower. When I touched the buds I found they were sticky, covered in resin the plant must have produced.

I walked through the room and found a hose lying coiled and plugged into a pipe. Turning the tap on the pipe to check if it was working, I sent an arc of water across the room, which hit the lights and made them sizzle briefly. I turned the tap back off as quickly as I could, but I felt reassured as I did so. I had water. I didn't know whether or not it was drinking water, but I had a stove; I could boil it. I would be all right for a while here. Now all I needed to find was a toilet. I coiled the hose back up as I'd found it, and walked on. Halfway down the left-hand wall I found another little side door. I looked through it, and saw a toilet and a sink glowing unnaturally, the enamel catching the blue light so that it seemed phosphorescent. I went into the room and tried the tap and found it worked, then examined the toilet and found it flushed. Then I went on and explored the rest of the bunker. There was no one else in there with me; just three rooms of plants growing under the blue lights, and then other sealed doors I couldn't prise open. I tried hammering against them with my fist, in case I could attract someone's attention, but heard nothing in response. I had thought perhaps I might be trapped in one part of a larger underground complex, and maybe there might be someone else trapped like me on the other side of those doors, but if there was they didn't hear me, or didn't come to investigate the banging. After a while I gave up and returned to the room with the window. The only clue I had to where I might be was the fact that the Chinese calendar pinned to the wall there was written in English.

I was hungry, and though I didn't want to accept the situation I was in, I decided that for all that I hated what was happening, I ought to be practical. So I filled the saucepan from the bathroom tap and returned it to the hob, and turned the hob on, and waited while the water heated up. There was no lid to the saucepan, and it seemed like for ever before I saw bubbles rising and could throw in the instant noodles. When they softened, I turned off the hob, found a pile of chopsticks by the bowls, and began to chew through the tasteless, rubbery noodles until they were gone. I tried to imagine a life where this was my only food source. It seemed unbearable. I took my bowl to the bathroom and rinsed it in the sink. I waited till the water in the saucepan that I'd used to cook the noodles was cool, then forced it down. It tasted foul, but it was quicker than boiling water all over again, and I didn't feel brave enough to try the water straight from the tap just yet. I put my bowl back with the other clean ones, and lay down on the roll mat, and tried to work out what to do. I ran my hands over my face, and knew something was wrong with it. The cheekbones felt different, the skin of my throat and my neck soft and clean-shaven, my hair too thick on my head. I knew I should go and look at my reflection in water, in the saucepan, in the bowl of the toilet. And yet I was simply too afraid of what was happening to me – I didn't want the answer. And when I looked at my hands, I still couldn't give voice to what it was that made them seem like the hands of a stranger. Wouldn't the same blockage rise up if I saw whatever face I was now wearing?

After twenty minutes with my head on the ragged pillow, I became too anxious to stay still any longer and got up, and for want of anything else to do, and because I felt unable to stay still, I went into the next room and picked up the hose and turned it on, then went round watering the plants. If I could keep them alive, perhaps I would stay alive too. Perhaps my life and the lives of the plants were linked somehow. I kept going through the three rooms until I found I had watered every row. When I had finished, a wave of exhaustion overwhelmed me. I supposed I had been awake for a long time now. I went back to the room with the window, and lay down once again on the roll mat, lying on my back and staring up at the plain concrete ceiling. Stress has a way of emptying people. I think I was asleep in less than a minute.

I found I couldn't sleep for long in there. I had no blanket, and although the heat of the electric lights meant I couldn't get very cold, the floor, being concrete, was hard and uncomfortable. It was getting darker when I woke that first time. I went to the calendar and examined it again, and it occurred to me that I ought to number off the days. Starting with the first day of the year on the calendar, I pressed an X into the paper with my thumbnail. Then I lay back down on the roll mat, and stared once more at the ceiling.

I pressed ten crosses into the calendar before I met another person. In that time, I sank into an exhaustion that meant I never felt fully awake, or fully asleep – I felt as if I was walking around drugged, as if something in the air had turned me into a zombie. I sank. Because I could only sleep for an hour or two at a time I was always tired, and the energy it took me just to heat up water and make noodles left me drained.

I couldn't work out how to escape, get home, get back to my wife, and that gave me the emptiest feeling. I tried to eat plenty of noodles to stay strong, but they had so little nutrition in them, I could feel my strength draining. Escape, get home, get back. To try and stay active, I carried on watering the plants every day. They didn't seem to be doing very well, and started to droop as the days rolled round, so I didn't think I was doing it right, but I did what I could and hoped I wouldn't be doing it for very much longer, that I would get out of here soon. On the third day, I threw a bowl at the window to try and break the glass, but the bowl hit the metal bars and shattered into shards. So I tried throwing the end of the hose at the glass instead, like a javelin, but I couldn't make it crack. I guessed it must be reinforced. By jumping and grabbing the bars and pulling myself up, I could take a closer look at it, but all I could see through it were the shadows of grass or leaves. I never turned the blue lights off, for fear I wouldn't be able to turn them on again and would be left there in the dark. And maybe you'll be surprised to hear this, but I never thought about killing myself, electrocuting or drowning or hanging myself with the hosepipe or the electrical cabling. I was going to get home. I tried to concentrate on that, even as my mind became weaker, even as I slipped into my drugged, somnambulant state. When I wasn't watering the plants I tried to exercise, do press-ups and sit-ups and star jumps to stay strong and alert, in case someone should come and I would need to break out of here past them. I never thought about killing myself. And I couldn't just lie on the mat all day.

I knew that before too long, I would have a visitor. Whoever had installed all these plants and was keeping all this electricity on would come and check on them at some point. I knew that would be my chance of getting out. So I slept on the roll mat, watered the plants, ate and drank and exercised and tried the locked doors every day, one after the other, then I would go to the toilet, wash up my cooking things and lie back down on the roll mat and wait, wait for someone to come and visit me. Under the weight of the tiredness that claimed me, my mind found its way to a kind of hibernation state. The thought of my flat and my job and my wife somewhere far from me was too painful to think about, so I found ways not to, or at least to keep it in the back of my mind. A lot of the time I cried. I dreamed of scenes of happiness that I had passed through in my old life, before this had happened, before I had lost myself; remembered times when things had been good, torturing myself with the happiness. I told myself that I would be all right. I had to, I simply had to believe that. I feared that if my faith were to falter for a moment, then I would lose all hope of ever finding a thread that could lead me out of the maze I'd wandered into.

Then, after ten days spent in the solitude and torpor of the bunker, crying, never really sleeping, never really waking, walking in circles round the cramped space and trying to be ready for someone to come, I had nodded off in the moment when the door opened and someone arrived from the outside world.

I heard the crunch of gravel and the mutter of an engine first, the world sounding faintly through the bunker window high above my head, but I didn't recognise it for what it was because it seemed to grow out of my dream, belong to the imagination. I dreamed whenever I lay down of my old life, the place I wanted to get back to and seemed powerless to stop myself drifting ever further away from as the days passed. So the engine and the gravel sounded to me like nothing more than a dream of freedom, and I didn't get up. Then I heard the bolt being drawn back on the bunker's main door, and realised almost too late what was happening, and scrambled to my feet. I went to the doorway to look into the hall, half hopeful, half afraid, angry at myself because I hadn't made a plan, wasn't carrying a weapon. It was dark in the entrance hall, and the blue light washing through from the strip lights further into the bunker made the place seem eerie. I stood in the doorframe, ready to dart back and hide, though I knew I couldn't hide for long in these empty quarters. The door opened and I caught a glimpse of the dark outside world, a rainy evening, England – surely it was England? The rich sucking smell of the muddy earth lit up in early moonlight and the sky losing memory of the sun and the day still clinging to everything; that in-between time when you can't put your finger on what the light reminds you of. Then figures came through the door towards me and I stepped away from them, back into the window room.

'He hasn't died then.'

They shut the door behind them once they were inside.

'All right, mate?' A man's head appeared round the doorway. 'Hiding, are you?'

He looked Chinese and spoke English with an English accent. He walked into the room where I was standing, quickly followed by a white man with a crew cut who was carrying two holdalls. As I watched, he opened the first holdall and tipped about a hundred packets of dried noodles over the floor.

'Provisions,' he said, looking at me. He had a strong southwest accent, Dorset or Somerset or somewhere like that. He smiled at me. 'Guess you're out of bog roll too, so I brought some of that, and some toothpaste. Don't say that we don't look after you.'

I didn't know what was going on, or who these men were, or who they assumed me to be. Clearly, they weren't surprised to find me here. Had they locked me in here on a previous occasion? Before I could form a question to put to them, a third figure came into the room – a young Asian boy, his eyes dull, his shoulders slumped, body cowled in a cheap tracksuit. He looked at me sullenly.

'We brought you a mate, mate,' the first man said. 'Thought you might need help keeping up with all the work – they need a lot of watering, don't they? You're lucky – we got one speaks your language.' Still I said nothing – I didn't know what he meant.

'Shall we go check?' The man with the crew cut lifted the other holdall over his shoulder and walked out into the main room where the lights were buzzing, radiating their heat. I followed him, desperate to speak but feeling too afraid, not knowing what questions I should start with. The other man came with me, but the Chinese boy stayed in the window room. We stopped in front of the wilting plants, and I cleared my throat.

'Excuse me?'

Neither man replied. They were staring at the plants. The man with the crew cut absentmindedly emptied his holdall in front of the bathroom, sending toilet rolls skittering over the floor, then stepped in among the plants to examine them more closely. He ran his hands over their tips and stems, then pulled off a leaf and crushed it and sniffed, and put some in his mouth and chewed it.

'He needs the help, all right.'

Without warning, I felt a fist crack against the back of my head and spun round, hurt, shocked, afraid. The other man was glaring at me.

'You've half killed them.' I raised my hand to my head. He'd caught me on my ear, and it stung from the blow. 'Gotta give 'em more water, all right?' He spoke very slowly, as if he thought I wouldn't understand. 'You work with your mate in shifts.' The two men turned abruptly and headed towards the second room of plants. I followed, still holding my hand to my ear.

'Look, what's going on?' I said. 'You can't keep me here. I don't want to be here.' The Chinese man looked back at me and shrugged.

'Don't understand you, mate,' he said. 'If you wanna talk then you have to learn English.'

He couldn't have heard me properly. Was there something wrong with him? Before I could speak again, the crew-cut man stopped in the doorway to the second room.

'It's all the same, but at least he hasn't fucking killed any of it,' he said. He walked back towards me and thrust his face into mine. 'You didn't listen proper when we told you what to do, did you? You haven't been doing enough!' I didn't speak, and avoided looking him in the eyes, hoping not to antagonise him. I didn't want them to hit me again. After a moment he stepped away from me, and kicked idly at a toilet roll that had rolled all the way across the room. 'But that's why we've brought your mate along, so don't worry. You'll cover it better between two.' He walked past me and started to head back towards the exit. 'Come on,' he called, 'we'd better go.' The Chinese man walked past me as well, and I followed them both, feeling panicked and desperate. This was my chance to get out. This was my chance to ask for help, and I was going to miss it; I was going to let it pass me by unless I did something now.

'Please, you have to let me out of here,' I said. The Chinese man didn't even look back at me as he spoke.

'Shut up, pal, and get on with your job. We'll be back in a week, all right?' I wanted to follow them out of the bunker, even if it meant being shunted into a different world and losing myself even further. I didn't care, I just wanted to get away from where I was. But the man with the crew cut turned and fixed me with a look when he got to the door, heaving it open behind him so I could see the night's coolness beyond him, the fresh air, the waiting Land Rover that would carry these two men away to wherever their lives went calmly on while mine was stalled and stolen from me.

'You try and rush me and I'll fucking kill you, you got that? I'll fucking kill you.' I stood and watched him, helpless as he turned and left. The two men closed and locked the door behind them. I heard them get into the Land Rover, and then the engine starting up. Its tyres moved angrily over the gravel, and then the sounds of my captors receded into the distance, into nothingness.

I stood alone in the entrance hall and wondered how I could have been so passive, so indecisive, so afraid. It was dark outside, and if I'd only got past them, I might have got away. I should have tried. Or I should have found a way to keep them here, to force them to listen to me, force them to understand. How could I have let so much simply happen to me, without taking any control?

I heard movement behind me and turned. The Chinese boy was standing in the doorway to the window room, watching me. For a moment I'd almost forgotten him. He seemed half sullen, half afraid, though I saw none of the shock in him that I was feeling. None of this seemed to surprise him at all.

'They've just left us here,' I said. 'How could they do that?'

The boy shrugged.

'They want us to water the plants, don't they.'

'But they can't just lock us up, that's illegal. I have a wife. I have a life elsewhere, they can't do this to me. People will be looking for me, they can't keep me here.'

The boy laughed and cocked his head to one side.

'What are you talking about?' he said.

'I'm telling you, something strange is happening to me, and I've become lost. I can't explain it properly but I'm lost. I don't understand it. I've been thrown into a different world. But I have a life waiting for me and I need to get home.'

The boy shook his head and looked at me with something like kindness, something like pity.

'I know how you feel,' he said. 'I feel the same. But look at you. You haven't got a wife. You don't have any job to go back to. I know it as well as you do. I know you. You're just another Vietnamese kid no one wanted, same as me.'

I stared at him, not knowing what to say. I looked at my hands. I raised my hands to my face, and realised that in all the days that had passed, I hadn't grown any stubble. I looked back at the boy.

'I need to sit down,' I said.

For the rest of that night, the boy told me his story. He wasn't Chinese, it turned out; he had been born into poverty in rural Vietnam thirteen years ago. When he was nine, a man had visited his village and spoken to everyone in the square, offering to arrange passage to England for boys and girls who wanted to work there and seek out a better life. The boy signed up and was trafficked into England in a cargo container with many other children of his age, from villages like his own. The boy was convinced that I must have been one of those children – maybe not in his container, but in another one like it.

'You must remember it, the hot dark and the days running one into each other, the water supply that we guarded and fought over? Sweating, pressed against the bodies of other children like us, all trying to break out of our cages, all believing this journey could release us into a better place? The way people took off layers of clothes to try and get cooler, the way our flesh would slip against the flesh of the people beside us, so we slipped back against the container walls? How the air tasted of rust and iron and tired, defeated fear? Don't you remember all the children like us having panic attacks, feeling the stabbing pains in our chests, desperately heaving the air into our lungs? All this must have happened to you just as it happened to me and hundreds of others like us, just as it is happening to people like us right now.'

I didn't know what to say and could only let him continue, listen to the memory bubble out of him like blood.

'Don't you remember hiding the tears when you thought of home and the things you had given up in the hope of something better? The love of your parents, the sun rising when you walked out to the fields to work? The shade of the trees when you sat down to rest and eat, and the feel of cool water on the back of your throat? I couldn't stop thinking of my grandparents as they sank into old age, and knowing I would not be with them when they died, and knowing I would never hear from them again, and perhaps never hear from my parents and brothers and sisters either, perhaps never return home, all because we had decided to follow these men who came to the village into the dark of this container, into the heat, into the unknown unimaginable wealth of England where everything would be different, where people would look after us, where we would lift ourselves up out of the lives we had been born to, and find peace in the sunlit uplands of secure employment. And perhaps one day we might find citizenship in this new country, and have all the security that would come with a new home, a better home. You must remember all this I'm telling you. It happened, I know it happened, and I know that it happened to you, didn't it?'

The container was unloaded at Southampton, and he had been put in the back of a lorry with a dozen other Vietnamese children. Perhaps, he said, I could have been one of them. From there, they were transported to the outskirts of a bigger city.

He was put to work for two years as a child prostitute in a house with blacked-out windows on a busy road where there didn't seem to be any shops, only one faceless ugly house after another. No neighbours ever seemed to go into their gardens. During the morning and afternoon rush hours the drive to the house would fill with cars, and cars would come and go from time to time throughout the day and night, and men would come into the house, always men, and he would wait in his bedroom. When he was alone, he watched the empty gardens through gaps in the sticky-back plastic covering the windows. None of the men could ever really look at him, and so he was always alone, most especially alone in the moments when there was someone else with him.

Some of the kids in the brothel were worn out quickly, unable to cope with the stress of what was happening to them, and they disappeared almost as suddenly as they came, vanishing after six months and never spoken of again. Others seemed to have been there for ever, and perhaps they might still be there even now, the boy said. How long you could last depended on your mental strength, and also on what physically happened to you. The boy's handler started talking about moving him on from that place when he'd been there half a year, but it was another eighteen months before he actually left. He never asked when he might be allowed out. He learned not to question anything. It was the best way to avoid beatings, and he was discouraged as well by the threats made against his family.

'If I said to someone that I was unhappy, or that I was tired, or I needed this to end, they would say to me, you owe us the cost of your passage to this country. We are going to let you begin a new life, in this country where there is so much for you. That is not worth nothing. You owe us a debt. If you cannot repay it, we will extract it from your family.'

'And they meant they would hurt them?'

He nodded.

'If I had ever run away, they would have killed them. Everyone they could find. They have the power at home; they can do that. No one will speak against them.'

'They can't just do what they want.'

He laughed.

'Maybe not,' he said, 'but no one stopped them trafficking all these young people out of the country and into these terrible lives we have been living. No one did anything. So I think they can do a lot.'

A time came when he was taken out of the brothel and transported to a different house with blacked-out windows, on the edge of an industrial estate. That house was filled with plants and bright lamps that helped them grow, and his job was to water them. He lived there alone, sleeping on a sofa in the hall because the bedrooms were filled with the plants and lamps. A handler visited him once a week to give him food and check his work, and sometimes to harvest the plants. He was told being alone represented a promotion, a great act of trust, and that he mustn't abuse it, or he would have to go back to the brothel. So he never tried to get out of the house. He just had to wait till he was allowed to go and find his own work and make his own way. It didn't matter so much – he didn't know where he would have gone if he'd left that building, even if he had had the courage. His handler explained to him that he had no rights in England, so the police wouldn't look after him. They would treat him worse than he was treated now, for sure; they were famous for it. There was no one he could go to for help.

Sometimes he would watch the lorries and vans and the occasional pedestrians who came and went from the industrial estate, and imagined one of them rescuing him, the childish fantasies of young boys all over the world, but he knew there would be nowhere for him to go, and he knew deep down that no one really cared. He comforted himself with the thought that even though he hated his solitude, it was better than the last place he'd been in. If he kept rising through the ranks like this, then before long he would surely earn his freedom and start to get paid, and even have the chance to leave, and then anything might be possible. There was still time, he was still young. He tried to cling to the thought that he had still done the right thing in coming to England. These first years had been terrible, but when he was a rich old man he would look back and know it was the right thing, and sacrifices had been necessary to get what he wanted. Nothing would have changed if he had stayed home and hungry in Vietnam, and one day things would happen for him here – he was sure of it, he believed it, he would not let it go. And so when he was told two weeks ago that he was being moved to a new site, and would be working with another boy to run a larger farm, he had taken it as a good sign that his plan was still on track.

'You're like me, you see. We're almost free. I think this is the end of our debt to them – I believe this is the last thing we have to do before we earn our freedom. It's the easiest task I have been put to yet – not alone as I was before, not abused as I was before that – all I have to do here is water the plants and try not to lose my mind, and make myself believe this locked door is normal and that in a little while it is going to open and I am going to be able to walk out of it into the light. I dream so much of seeing the sun, and walking out into woods somewhere, and being in the fields and working. I dream of my family, still back at home in the fields where perhaps my grandparents have died by now. Perhaps my brothers and sisters no longer miss me – I want so much to be like them once more, free in the light of the day to work at what suits them, free to go wherever they want as long as they're home for dinner. I didn't get to be young for very long and I would like to be young again.'

Gently, I tried to explain to him that he had it wrong. He was a victim of human trafficking, and would never be freed by these people while they could still make money out of him. But when I told him my own story, he told me I was mad, and wouldn't listen to anything else I said to him, so we fought, then agreed to disagree.

'I can see why you wouldn't believe me,' I told him.

'Can you.'

'Of course I can. It's hard to explain so that it makes sense to you. But it's true, all the same.'

'I think maybe we just shouldn't talk about it.'

So I stopped, and we didn't talk about very much, and after a while he lay down to sleep, and I followed his example.

The next morning we started working harder at watering the plants. We took turns to rest on the roll mat, or go round the bunker with the hose. The boy was more zealous than I was, and got impatient with me when I didn't water them properly. He tried drinking water straight from the tap, and didn't get sick, so I stopped boiling my water before I drank it. We helped each other scramble up and look out of the window at the shadows of the leaves beyond, and tried to break the glass, but found we still couldn't. We couldn't get the bars loose either. I realised I would have to escape through the door, if I was going to escape at all. As the days passed, the plants started to look healthier. We fell into a rhythm of telling each other stories when we were both awake, making up stories to get each other through the long nights as they seemed to grow a little colder.

When a few days had passed, I started to talk to him about the idea of escaping. We couldn't just break out through the window, so I knew we needed to come up with some smarter plan.

'You have to see, we can't stay here. This is intolerable, and we need to get away from this place, we need to get out before the hearts go out of us and we don't have the strength to try and resist them any more.'

He didn't want to hear me, shook his head, blocked his ears.

'I don't want to listen to you.'

'Why?'

'You're dangerous. You're here to test me. I'm not going to listen.'

'Why don't you want to get away from here?'

'My family. I told you. They would hurt my family.'

'They're not really going to hurt your family. They don't remember where you're from, they haven't kept a record. It's just something they say to control you.'

He didn't want to hear me.

'You don't know that! What if you're wrong?' He slapped both palms against the concrete floor, the sound ringing sharp through the air between us, his eyes boring into me. 'I've known people whose families were hurt because they let things go wrong. You can't say that doesn't happen – it does, it does, it happens all the time, it happens to everyone.'

I couldn't explain to him that because this wasn't really my life, because this wasn't really happening to me – I was only trapped in someone else's problem – his worries didn't weigh so heavily on me. He didn't believe me, of course, and it just made him angry. And it felt too cruel to say it to him as openly as that.

'But you can't seriously want to spend the rest of your life in this place?'

'I won't. I will work here and gain their trust and they will keep offering me promotions.'

'It's not true. They're not going to let you go, they're lying to you.'

The boy laughed.

'Maybe. But if I have to choose who to believe, I'm going to believe them over the boy who tells me he's actually a white man with a wife who's been trapped in someone else's body. It's not much of a choice, but I'm not going to believe you first.'

I went to the bathroom and filled up cups with water for both of us to drink, walking away from him for a minute to let myself calm down, to try to work out how to explain my situation to him. I came back and gave him the water, then sat down opposite him and tried to lay things out as simply as possible.

'Look. I'm going to try and escape. It would be easier if we both tried to do it together, but I understand if you don't want to do that. But you cannot try to stop me from escaping. Understand?'

The boy looked at me, and again it was with something like pity that he took me in.

'Let's say the nonsense you tell me is true,' he said. 'Let's say you are trapped in someone else's body. OK. Have you thought about whose body it is you're in? Have you thought about his family, and what will happen to them if you force him to escape like this? Because someone will be killed, either you or a relative; someone will be killed if you run away from them. They have to set the example.'

I hadn't thought about whose body I was in, not really. I realised once he asked me that up till now I had still been thinking of this as a kind of dream I was trapped in, not some other reality, as real to this boy as the reality I had left behind. It made me uncomfortable, but I tried to push the thought away. Very simply, this couldn't be real life, because real life was governed by the laws of physics and logic and things like that, and I was living outside all that, so none of what I was experiencing could really be happening. It was important I remembered that. If I didn't, I would be lost; I would forget where I'd come from. Then I would never find the way to get home. I'd end up trapped in a bunker like this one for ever.

'I can see you're not going to go along with me on this,' I said. 'But I still need you to promise not to try and alert them, if I try to escape. Can you do that? It will go badly for you if you try and tell them.'

The boy laughed.

'And you think it won't go badly for me if you do escape, and they realise I could have tried to warn them?'

'We'll make it look like you couldn't have told them, if that helps you. You could be watering the plants when they come, at the far end of the bunker. You don't have to be anywhere near the door.'

'And what is your plan? Just to rush them when they open the door, is that it? And hope you surprise them – is that all the plan you have?'

'If you're not coming with me, you don't need to know.' I didn't say any more to him then, because he knew as well as I did that that was all the plan I could possibly have: there was no other way of getting out. I would just have to try to get past them, then outrun them. With luck, they would visit in the dark again, and that would give me a better chance of getting away from them once I was outside. But that was all the idea that I had, and it seemed so fragile, I didn't want to talk about it, in case looking at it too closely made it fall apart.

When I wasn't watering the plants, I gave some thought to this question the boy had put into my mind. Could this be someone else's real life? Might the body I was in be a human soul, a life with loved ones and sorrows they carried with them just as I did?

The idea came to me that I must be ill in some way. There is a border where your mind meets the world, interprets all the stimuli around it, gives them some order so it can understand its surroundings and the world it's in, and that border can fracture and break down very easily. That starts with daydreaming, with taking yourself somewhere else in the middle of the day, the simple way we all have of combating boredom or escaping from stress. For some people, though, that experience goes further. Some people who have lived through terrible things will start believing the world isn't really happening to them; that the world is a dream, or that someone else is dreaming them, that these are not their real lives and things are not as they seem. Some people under stress will enter fugue states, where they lose some of the bricks that have made up their identity till then, some of their memories, some of their basic traits. I have met people who became different people, or started to speak in several voices, because something terrible had happened to them.

I couldn't persuade the boy to escape with me, but he did agree, very fearfully, to look the other way while I made my attempt. He would go to the far end of the bunker and water the plants as soon as we heard a car approaching. In the whole of the week that we waited for the men to return to us, we had no false alarms – no other vehicles came within earshot, and he wouldn't try a practice run, but I tried not to worry about him. I had other preparations to make.

The day before the men were due to come back, I unplugged one of the lamps in the first room of plants, and propped it up against the wall in the entrance hallway.

'What are you doing?' the boy asked.

'I have to create a distraction when they come in. I need a weapon.'

'That's too big. It'll be too heavy. You'll swing it once and then they'll kick you to death, and they'll leave you dead in here with me. They'll use you for fertiliser, my friend.'

'I'm only going to need to swing it once.'

I relied on the fact that they wouldn't want to kill me. I knew if I failed I'd have my head kicked in, but as far as I knew it was always difficult to get rid of a body no matter who you were, and these men wouldn't want the hassle of it. So I hoped that if the worst came to the worst and I didn't escape, I would suffer a few broken ribs, and then the next week I would be able to try again. And besides, in the back of my mind was the thought that if I could just get through the open door, the same strange trick would be played on me again, and I would find myself in a different world, and wouldn't need to worry about this body and this place I was in right now. So I leant the lamp against the cold concrete wall, and waited for the Land Rover's approach.

They came late at night, but I was awake, and shook the boy awake as soon as I heard them.

'What is it?' He rubbed his eyes, bleary, hostile.

'They're here.'

He looked at me through frightened eyes, and I saw he was too afraid to break out of the situation he had been placed in. And I wished I could help him, but he had refused to run. There was no more I could do; I had to harden my heart and leave him.

'You're really going to go through with it?'

'I have to.'

He rubbed his eyes again, childlike and blinking where he sat on the floor.

'You should come with me.'

He shook his head.

'It's not worth it. It's not worth the risk.'

'What if I get out?'

'You won't. And even if you did, they'd kill your family.'

'All right. Your choice. Then you have to promise not to do anything. Don't tell them what's happening, don't alert them. OK?'

He looked away from me and I grabbed his arm, wrenching him round to keep looking at me.

'Let go of my arm.'

'You have to promise.'

He grinned, sullen. He knew they were out of the car now, and approaching the front door; he knew that we only had moments.

'Or what?'

'Please. Just stay quiet, that's all.'

His shoulders slumped, and I let go of him.

'All right. I won't say anything. And I hope you get to where you want to go.'

'You could come with me,' I tried one last time.

'I'm going by a different route,' he said, and shrugged as if he was apologising.

I left him then. I should have tried to ease the fear in him, I should have cared more for him, because then I could have encouraged him to believe in me, believe the plan could work, and then perhaps I could have helped him get out of this life he was in as well. But it was too late now. I had to go ahead on my own.

My plan was very simple; I had tried to think of different options but in reality there were none. I picked up the lamp I had left in the hallway, and waited by the front door. I soon heard them approaching on the other side, followed by the rattle of the door being unlocked. I waited. It seemed there were several keys involved in the process. I waited, legs shaking, feeling afraid, feeling elated. The door started to roll back. I saw the night beyond it open up its smile, unmapped and inviting. Then a hand took hold of the bunker door and started levering it open. I stepped round the corner of the door, and swung the lamp as hard as I could up into the face of the white man who had done most of the talking the last time, who was holding the door and closest to me. I caught him on the jaw and spun him round. His hand shot to his face, and I saw fear in his eyes for a moment before he realised what had happened, then I saw anger flooding through him. The other man was standing behind him, and for a moment couldn't reach me past his friend. For a split second, none of us did anything but register each other. Then I threw the lamp at both men and ran.

The first thing I noticed, to my panic, was that the world hadn't changed simply because I'd left the bunker; I hadn't found myself translated into some new environment – the shouts of the men behind me were the same voices I had heard the previous week. Whatever strange magic had taken me over for a moment and brought me to this place seemed to have stopped working, and I was going to have to escape my captors for real. I would have to outrun them, hide from them, get away from them through this night. As my legs started pumping and I began to cross the open ground around the entrance to the bunker, heading for a line of trees about thirty feet away, it occurred to me that perhaps I was trapped in this life now, this body. Surely that couldn't be possible, could it? I couldn't have turned for ever into this new human being whose skin I was in?

But there wasn't time to worry about that now. For as long as I still had to outrun these men, that was all I could focus on. I had to run. I had to burst my lungs wide open.

The land around the bunker was more open than I had hoped. Deciduous woodland scrabbled away from me for a little while, lining a dirt track that seemed to lead to freedom, but I was surprised to see through the trees that we were in farming country, surrounded by ploughed fields. Whatever that bunker was, it wasn't hidden in some unmapped wild, we were close to civilisation. I risked a look back over my shoulder as I ran. Only the Vietnamese man was chasing me; my heart leapt. Either I had hurt the other one badly, or else he was preoccupied with the other boy inside the bunker, and rushing to check the plants. Outrunning only one man seemed simpler than outrunning two of them. I crashed through the trees by the side of the road, tripping on brambles and undergrowth but managing not to lose my feet from under me completely. It occurred to me suddenly that the other man might be getting back in the Land Rover; if I could make it as difficult as possible for him to follow me, keep away from the roads, then that would increase my chance of survival.

My breath was coming to me raggedly now, my lungs burning. I gritted my teeth and started running over the undulations of the field. If it hurt me to fly through the night like this, perhaps it hurt the man pursuing me. Perhaps I could wear him down before too long.

At the bottom of the field I saw denser woodland and recognised the scrubby treeline that tends to mark out the path of a river. For a moment I was alarmed; would I find myself pinned against the water? Would he catch up with me there? I looked behind me again and saw I had pulled further away from the man, who was back at the start of the field and moving heavily now. Perhaps the river would play in my favour. If I could just get across it, and he was far enough behind, and his lungs burned like mine did, then perhaps that would be the moment when he gave up chasing? I turned again, staggering on the uneven ground, and tried to accelerate towards the trees, keep going, keep pumping, blood and air coursing through me. In another moment I reached the shadow of the trees, the green life that had sprung up around the water, and tried to make out the river. What I didn't see, though, was a root jutting out from a hawthorn tree. My foot was suddenly caught, and I felt my stomach turn over as I was hurled off course and through the air. I saw the water then, as I flew towards it, saw the nettles and the bracken as I passed through them towards the edge of a little stream flowing down in between the trees. I didn't have time to brace myself for impact; I landed on my left shoulder, my knees grazing against something hard and cold, so I cried out as I was thrown down into the water. I tried to hold my breath as I landed head first in the stream.

Then suddenly everything around me was changed. I felt the shift in my body at once; I could tell I had become heavier and older than I had been a moment ago. Even as I made this observation, someone kicked me in the small of my back, and I was propelled forwards once again on to my hands and knees. My right hand started to bleed, and I saw I had grazed it against a stone. I looked around to see who was behind me, who had kicked me, to work out whether I had passed into a different world or whether the same man had now caught me up. Behind me was a man standing by the open door of a saloon car, and beyond him, the night stretching away from us for miles. It was dark, and we were somewhere high up, surrounded by a view of fields and the lights of roads and villages. Unmistakably, I was in a different place. I took the image in for a moment before my focus turned to scrabbling away from the man as he walked towards me. He looked to be in his fifties, running to fat but still a strong-looking man, thunder on his face as he closed in on me. He grabbed me by the throat and aimed a punch at my teeth. The impact sickened me as I felt pain dart through my tongue, tasted blood in my mouth.

'Where is she?'

'I don't know what you mean,' I said, except that my voice wasn't clear – my tongue was swelling up and it was painful to speak. The man hit me again, on the cheekbone.

'You're gonna tell me.'

'Please, you need to listen to me.' He hit me again, in the stomach this time, and I doubled over as I felt the air go out of me. I tried to breathe in, but my lungs wouldn't take anything. For a moment I panicked, feeling the blood rushing through my body, hearing it pound in my ears. The man squatted down in front of me, placed a hand against my shoulder and pushed me back. I watched him as I fought to get air back into my lungs. 'I don't know who you're looking for,' I said. I tried to concentrate on the man's face, but my mind was racing. How had

I passed from the other place to this one? Could it be that it wasn't just walking through doors that did this to me? Was it possible that falling into the water had dislocated me from the last world in just the same way? That passing from one state to another – through a door, through a different element like water – I was plunged into a different world? I wondered for an instant whether the boy I had been till moments ago was still out in that field somewhere, and what might be happening to him now, whether he had been caught once he had fallen over, whether the violence inflicted on him as a result would somehow now happen to me as well.

'Stop fucking about now, all right?' the man said. 'I know who you are. I know who you are. Look at me. The post mortems on the last two showed they were still alive two days after capture. So where have you taken her, where is she hidden?' He waited for a heartbeat, for a breath, waited for me to say something while I took in the gravity of what I had just heard. Then he started to hit me again, all his strength hammering into my face, my mouth, my nose. I felt my nose break, a blossoming of pain that made me cry out.

I tried to understand what was happening to me. This man suspected me of murders. How could I tell him I was someone else? How could I show him he was attacking the wrong man? The boy in the bunker hadn't believed me; why would anyone else?

But even as I wondered how to explain my situation, another thought came to me, a dim and uneasy image that seemed to surface as if from a swamp in the darkest recesses of my brain. I remembered the wood I had found myself in when this nightmare had first started. The tall silent trees, the needles underfoot, the endless walk I had embarked on, thinking I would be able to get back home. And out of that memory, another one that couldn't possibly have been mine seemed to grow, like buds on a branch, like an organ turning cancerous and swelling into view on a scan. The image came to me of items of women's clothing – shoes, dresses, handbags, tops – buried under the needles in that wood. I didn't know what it meant. I didn't know whether it could have anything to do with me. All I knew was that the image made me feel sick. The thought of all those shoes buried deep in the forest was suddenly in my mind and I could not erase it, I could not shut it out, and it was more painful than the fist in my face, my broken nose.

Could it be possible that I was in the body of a man who had done something terrible? And if I was, then was I in some way responsible for what he had done? Did his guilt flow on into me now I was here and taking the beating?

The man crouching over me rained blows down on my head. I tried to shield myself with my hands, but it achieved little. He hit me in the ribs, and I felt one crack. He stood and started to kick me in the legs, the balls, the stomach. I curled up, foetal, and tried to imagine myself away from him. He stopped, breathing heavily. I didn't look up.

'Where are we?' I asked him.

'What?'

'Where are we?'

'Why does it matter?'

I looked up at him and found my left eye was swelling up. I could barely see out of it. I worried I was losing my vision. Was it just swelling, or was the eye itself damaged?

'I don't know where I am.'

The man rubbed at the stubble on his chin.

'Danebury. You're on Danebury hill fort. There's no one to hear you. So you need to talk.'

I looked around through my one good eye at the night. So here we were, atop a hill fort of all places, alone and marooned high above the soil in the hollow middle of Wiltshire, a county many miles from anywhere, a county I only knew at all because my wife had happened to grow up there. It was painful in that moment to be reminded of my wife.

'I don't know what you want me to say.'

'Tell me where she is. Tell me where you've hidden her and this can stop. I'll take you down the station and this can stop.'

I frowned, confused by what he'd said.

'So you're a police officer?'

He aimed another kick at my stomach.

'Of course I'm a fucking police officer. Don't get smart. Concentrate on what you need to be telling me.'

My mind raced. Clearly, this man must be out on a limb. He had picked me up somewhere and driven me out here, to an abandoned hill fort in the country, determined to beat the shit out of me till I told him where I had hidden some woman. It dawned on me for the first time that a woman might be in pain somewhere, hidden somewhere, alive somewhere, that she might need saving. Was there a way I could help her? If a memory of buried things could come to me that didn't seem to be my own, was there a way I could work out where she was, and help this man, and end this beating?

'Where did you arrest me?' I asked. The police officer leaned down, almost casually, and punched me again in the face. I saw blood on his knuckles. Already, the flesh of my face was being transformed like magic into pulp. It was so easy to tear apart the fabric of a human being.

'You fucking know where I fucking arrested you.'

'Just say it. Just say where you found me.' I took a breath, and took a risk. 'How close are we to the Savernake Forest?'

The police officer stared at me intensely.

'Are you fucking brain damaged or something? Do you not remember anything? We're down the road, it's over there – come on, you know that.'

So I was right: I was here again, I had come back here somehow. But had I stepped back into the body of the man in the middle of the woods? I steeled myself to ask another question.

'Did you arrest me at a services? Was I in a service station cafe?'

'Fuck's sake, you know you were. What are you playing at?' He slapped me this time, an open palm against my face, and I worried my eardrum had broken.

It had to be the same story I had found my way back into. I had to be the same man. I had walked out of that wood and driven to those services, and gone inside, and then this man had come and found me and taken me up this hill, convinced I knew where a woman was dying, convinced, I guessed, that he could save her if he acted quickly enough. I had to be the same man. So why had I gone out into those woods? Could it be that something had happened out there, that I had done something terrible? Could it be that this woman was waiting out there now?

There was no point keeping the thought to myself. So far, I hadn't stayed trapped in any of the lives I had visited. Unless, I supposed, I counted the years I had spent in the one I thought of as my own; unless that first life was no more real than this one. So that meant I would most likely be able to escape this scene at some point. I would pass through a doorway, through water, perhaps even out of shadow and into light, some liminal moment where things seemed to be changing, and find myself shunted again into some other story. I would get away from the gravity of this situation and find a moment's silence, find the time to work out what had happened to me, and how I could stop it. So if

I knew I would be able to get away from all this at some point, then it must be my duty to try to find this woman I had hidden somewhere out in the woods.

'I think I can help you,' I said. The officer rocked back on his heels, startled, alert.

'Yeah?'

'The Savernake Forest. I think she's out there somewhere in the woods.'

'You think?'

'You're not going to understand, but it wasn't me who did this. I don't know about this, but I think she's out there. I think there are clothes buried out there as well.'

'Clothes?'

'Yeah. I don't know, like trophies.'

'Buried clothes for trophies.'

'There have been other victims?'

He looked at me closely now.

'You're seriously telling me you don't remember?'

'Were there other victims? Besides this woman who's missing?'

He took a deep, unhappy breath of the night air.

'Yes. Two other women.'

'Were they buried?'

'No. They were found in the Savernake.'

So that was where I went to do my work.

'I think it's the clothes that were buried instead,' I said. 'I think he doesn't want to keep the bodies, he wants to keep the clothes.'

'*You* want to keep the clothes, you mean.'

'I don't know. I don't know, maybe.'

The policeman watched me carefully, hostile, angry, ready to reject what I was saying. But something had rung true with him; something had made sense.

'Why not the bodies? Why just the clothes?'

I didn't know what to say. Then a thought occurred to me and I spoke before I understood its meaning.

'Maybe the lives aren't there any more. Maybe those lives are gone and he has to move on to new ones.'

The police officer continued to watch me, cautious, appraising. At last he spoke again, after what felt like a long silence.

'So you're saying she's in the Savernake somewhere.'

Now, I thought, he was about to start beating me up again, because I didn't know where in the woods this woman was, I didn't know what had happened to her. He would ask me to narrow things down, and I wouldn't be able to, and then the violence would start all over again, unless I thought of a way to avert it.

'I can take you to where the car was parked,' I said, suddenly realising there was still something I knew that could be of use to him.

'What car?'

'Look, I don't know anything about this. But I know I found myself in the middle of those woods, and then I got in a car and drove away from them, and then I walked into a service station and now I'm here, and I can at least take you back to the place where I started.'

The policeman checked his watch.

'Is this an amnesia you're talking about?'

I wished I could tell him what I was really going through right now, the full story of what was happening to me. But that wouldn't have made any sense to him; he wouldn't have listened. And he wouldn't be able to help me, even if I did get the story through to him. Whatever had happened was a deeper and more fundamental fracture than one police officer was going to be able to heal, I felt sure. I hoped with all my heart that this was some kind of dislocating violence my mind was doing to me, and that if I sat down for long enough with some psychiatrist or psychologist or whoever's job it was to solve mysteries like these, I might find my way home to my own life. The alternative – that this was some magic, that this was really happening – was too terrible to contemplate.

'It doesn't matter now. I can take you to where the car was parked, is that something?'

The policeman nodded curtly.

'All right,' he said, 'that's a start. Get up and get in the vehicle.' I levered myself to my feet, my arms and legs and the small of my back aching from the kicks and blows he had ploughed into them. He stood still and silent, and watched me as I walked to the car that had brought us up here to this hill fort, and opened the back door. Before I got in, I paused to take a breath of fresh air. Calm fell on me momentarily as I looked out at the night around. My head was aching, but the adrenaline in my body kept me from feeling too much pain yet. I looked out over the lights of the villages and filled my lungs, and felt it was the first fresh breath of air I had taken in weeks, since I had found myself trapped underground in the bunker. I looked out over the lights. The eerie feeling came to me that this was my life, no matter how impossible that might seem. This moment was my life, and when I died, it would be what had happened to me while I was breathing. This was not just some interlude, some break – it was a moment of my living, part of all the rest. The cool of the night and the dark, watchful land around me made me feel so much freer than I had done since the moment I'd found myself in the wood, and though I thought it was madness to have sunk so low, this, for an instant, felt almost like happiness, to be breathing out, to be breathing in.

Then I became afraid. I was growing accustomed to things, I was accepting this non-reality, and I must not do that, I couldn't let that happen or I'd never get away from it. I had to fight this nightmare I was in. It was the only way of waking up. Till that happened, I couldn't let myself stop and relax and breathe in the night air. I turned away from the view and got into the back of the car, and the police officer got into the front, and the engine started.

'What's your name?' I called through the grille between us. He didn't turn round to look at me. He didn't reply.

We drove through the night, down quiet Wiltshire roads, until the roadsides were swallowed in forest and trees and I guessed we had reached the edge of the Savernake. The police officer flicked glances at me in the rear-view mirror, not trusting me for a moment, not yet believing what I had said.

'Where should we go then?' he asked me.

I wondered how to describe it.

'What I know is that I came out of the woods by driving down a long mud track – a Land Rover track, not a proper road. And then I kept on a straight line pretty much till I reached the service station. So if we were to follow that road, we'd see it.'

'You don't know any more than that?'

'I'm sorry. That's all I remember.' We drove on a little, the car's radio crackling with messages from time to time. I couldn't quite hear what they were saying. 'I guess no one knows that we're out here, do they?' I said.

'Why do you say that?'

'If someone knew you'd taken a suspect out to the middle of nowhere and beat the shit out of him, we'd be driving back to the station, and you'd be writing off your pension.'

He watched me in the mirror.

'Sometimes you have to put your pension second. If she's still alive, I'll be happy with what I've done.'

'Will you?'

'Of course.'

I shrugged.

'If you saved someone this time, maybe that would be a good thing. But what about the next time, when it doesn't work, and you break someone's neck? What about the next bloke?'

The man laughed.

'I don't need lectures from you,' he said.

'Suit yourself.' I could see he was uncomfortable. I didn't know how he had found me, whether we had met before, what chain of events had led him to picking me up as he had, and doing what he'd done, but I could guess well enough that he'd acted in anger, and I was sure he must be worried that he'd made the wrong decision. 'I guess you'll just have to see what your superiors say, won't you.'

'That's right.'

'And whatever lawyer ends up representing me. I guess you could get a case kicked out of court for this kind of coercion of a suspect pretty easily.'

'Not with three bodies lined up as evidence you won't,' he spat, and I saw real fear behind the teeth he had bared at me. He had done the wrong thing and realised it too late, and now he was counting out the consequences. His eyes flicked back to the road. 'What about this?' he said. 'What about here?' I looked out of the window, and saw a track leading down among the trees away from the tarmac. It seemed familiar.

'That might be it,' I said. 'Let's try it out.'

We turned off the road and started down the dark track, head-lights revealing a world of stark shadows, the black and white and light and dark of crime and ghosts and nightmares, the gleam of secrets, the eyes of animals watching us. We came to the end of the track, and I knew it was the same place. For a moment I felt strangely close to him, perhaps even sorry for him. He had realised somewhere along the road we had just driven down that his career was over; he had done something stupid and there would be no stepping back from it. The state I was in spelled the end for him. Now the only way he could make that worthwhile was to find this woman alive somewhere in this deep, dense woodland in the middle of the night, this dark wood I had shouted out into the last time I had come here, hearing no one, hearing no movement. I felt certain there was no one here. But he needed to find someone, or he would have just thrown his career away for no reason. There was something heroic about it. Something sad and tragic, like a movie. Though the pain in my body was starting to come into focus as the exhilaration of the attack left me, I still felt sorry for the doomed man in the front seat whose fatal flaw was about to claim him.

'Get out,' he said.

So I did, and he too swung quickly to his feet, tense and nervous. I pulled myself upright and looked at him.

'This is where I started,' I told him.

He looked at me, eyes narrowed.

'What do you mean?'

'I found myself in the middle of this wood, and everything's been wrong since. So I don't know whether what you're looking for is going to be out here. But this is where things went wrong for me.'

The man turned round and looked out into the trees where the car lamps lit them.

'Is she out there?' he asked.

'I don't know. We can only look.' In the back of my mind, I wondered whether there might be other things waiting to be found out there. Doorways back into the world I had come from; clues for how I could get out of this present, back into my past. I hoped if we walked out into that forest, we both might find something we wanted in there. 'Do you want me to walk ahead of you?'

He turned back to me, nodding slowly, working out what was going on. He didn't trust me, of course; I could see he was suspicious. And it was natural he would be – I was a murder suspect, helping him look for the body. How often did that happen? He must have been wondering at my motivation, half convinced I was mad.

'Go on then,' he said, so I walked past him and out into the floodlit land before us, savaged and scarred by the shadows of the pines. My own shadow stretched out ahead of me, vast and looming in the car lights, like a ghost that was leading my way. I wondered whether he might know where we were going, the ghost. Whether he might be the rest of me, guiding my steps.

We walked for a minute, and then it was dark again, the car lights no longer doing any good.

'Hang on.'

I stopped and turned around. He must have been concerned I would try to run away. I supposed that if I could outrun him, there would be a chance of escaping. But I didn't want to rush through these woods; I wanted to comb every inch of them. Couldn't there be a portal out here somewhere that could take me home? He took a torch out of his pocket, and shone the beam at first into my eyes so that I had to hold up my hands to cover them.

'We'll walk together now,' he said. He stepped forward and stood beside me, both of us breathing deep lungfuls of forest air, trying to nose our way to a clue, a sense of what direction we ought to be going in.

'That way, maybe,' I said, and set off at random, heading away from the car. I no longer remembered anything about the walk I had taken through this place, and it was too dark to look for tracks or footprints. I would just have to follow my nose.

Or I supposed I could try and treat this walk through the dark woods, looking for a way out, looking for a body, as an exercise in divination, and see if that helped me to think any clearer. If I really was in the body of a man who had killed someone and hidden the body round here, then what seemed like a logical hiding place to me might well be the correct location. It seemed to have been me who chose it in the first place, after all.

I picked my way through the dark's soft loam, hoping the night would give up some of its secrets. The police officer walked at my side, flashing his torch all around us. I tried to take in my surroundings, to let them shape the way I walked, but no buried memory came to me of things I might have done out here, while it hadn't been me who inhabited this body. I was alone in the dark, and guessing, and that was all there was to it in the end. But I stayed quiet, and thought that for a good while, if I didn't show the uncertainty I was feeling, the man by my side might trust me, and we might keep walking, and one of us might discover something by chance. I searched everywhere for signs of some kind of portal to another world, some way back to the place I had come from. I didn't know what such a thing would look like – a door, a bright light shining. There was no way to tell. My head cleared for the first time in a long time, as I realised no one was chasing me, no one was hitting me, I wasn't in any physical danger, and I felt very keenly the anguish of injustice that had been in me all this time since things had gone wrong, waiting for me to confront and examine it. There was also the small boy's fear and the shocked, bruised, emotional vulnerability of having been thrust out of my life into bright and unknown light. Really, all I wanted to do was get home to my wife and hold her, and be held by her, and I didn't know what I had done wrong to deserve this, I didn't know why I no longer deserved to be with her. I felt afraid. Why had this happened to me? Who was going to make it better?

'Is any of this familiar to you?' the officer said.

'I don't know.'

'You don't know?'

'I don't remember any of the things you think I've done. I didn't do them. I'm just trying to trust my instinct and see where it might lead.'

He stopped walking and waited for a moment, and then sighed deeply.

'So we're just wandering round in the woods?' he said.

I wished I could tell him there was more to it than that, but there were no words to make him understand.

'We're just seeing what we find, yes.'

He nodded. He didn't want to turn back, of course. I felt for him, as I watched him weighing up his limited and disappearing options. All that was happening to me seemed like a dream, but it was his life, it was important to him, it was the most important thing in the world to him. He sighed heavily, and I saw that he had given up.

'This is ridiculous. I have no idea whether she's out here. I have no idea whether you're being honest with me. We need to turn back for the station.'

'I'm being honest with you.'

'Why would I believe a word you say?'

I knew there was no point in arguing. If I could have shown him who I really was, shown him the story so he believed the whole truth of it, maybe then things would have been different. But I couldn't see a way.

'All right,' I said.

The police officer cast his eyes out into the dark of the forest one last time.

'There's no one out there, is there?' he said, almost under his breath, as if talking to himself. I was struck by the strange inversion of the moment – how many people had ever walked through a wood at night, hoping to stumble upon a dead body? Everything was upside down. He stepped forward and gestured for me to start walking. 'Come on,' he said, 'back to the vehicle.'

I wanted to comfort him. Wanted to tell him he'd done his best, and I would have helped if I'd known how to help him. But I was the enemy, and everything I said was only making him trust me less. I had done my bit; I had brought us here, and we had tried. But neither of us had found what we were looking for, and now it was time to turn back. We reached the car and got in and he sighed again, and I thought that was the sound of the heart going out of him. We reversed out of the wood, and the trees lit up by the headlamps seemed to be running to keep up with us, the lights always lagging a little way behind. When we were back on the road we drove quickly, and he called in to the station to let them know he was bringing a suspect in.

We came to the edge of some town, the street lights looming over us like herons, and then the lights of a police station were filling the windscreen, filling the field of my vision. I felt nothing as the car stopped and the officer stepped out and pulled my door open. It wasn't my life to feel panicked about. It wasn't my tragedy to pity. I couldn't quite believe what was happening was real, so I felt numb. Or was it that everyone who kills someone kills a bit of themselves at the same time, shuts a door on some part of themselves that they never reopen, and the numbness in me was really the numbness of the body I was trapped in? The officer stood over me, pinning me to the side of the car before we went inside.

'I think I could lose my job over what I've done to you this evening,' he said. His eyes were on my lip. I darted out my tongue, and found my lip was bleeding. 'I just want you to know that I don't regret it. I just want you to know that I'd do it again.'

I didn't say anything. I couldn't see any point. My mind had been claimed now by a different anxiety. We turned and started to walk towards the building, and my eyes focused on the entrance door. I realised with sudden clarity that the scene was about to change again, that everything was about to become different once more, and that in five seconds I would walk through that doorway and out of this moment. There was no room in me to engage with this man. All my fears focused on what world I was about to be hurled into. We walked up the few steps to the entrance of the police station, bright light narrowing our eyes as the doors swung open. I held my breath. Then we passed through the doorway, and I wasn't there any more.

I was lying in a ditch by the side of a road, and next to me was the woman I had seen in the caravan. We were both wearing waterproofs, head to toe, resting our heads on Karrimor rucksacks, and I was freezing, and I could see in the way the woman wrapped her arms around her body that she was too. I stared at her. She didn't lash out; she didn't speak either. This woman was different from the other people I had encountered till now. There was kindness in her, gentleness. I wondered whether there might be a different way of talking to her; some way of finding out where I was and who I was that wouldn't have been possible in the other worlds I had passed through on my journey.

'I've forgotten where we are,' I said, watching her carefully, trying not to say anything that would alarm her too much. The expression on her face, pinched and pale with the cold, barely changed.

'We're inland from Dover,' she told me.

I nodded.

'I've forgotten why we came here.'

'We're going to the cliffs, you remember? The view of the ocean.'

I took a deep breath, took a risk.

'I've forgotten who we are.'

She frowned now, alarmed, a little afraid of what was happening. 'What?'

'Who are we? I don't remember.'

The woman peered at me, afraid, uncertain.

'It's us.'

'You're my wife?' I asked her, hoping this might be the answer. She laughed, a high laugh, like something taking flight, hardly human.

'I'm your sister.'

I nodded, confounded, trying to cover it.

'I'm sorry. I think that it's the cold. I know that. You're my sister. I think that it's the cold.'

She started to lever herself to her feet.

'Come on then,' she said to me, 'let's get moving.'

I stood up and looked around me as we shouldered our backpacks. We were by the side of a quiet country road. The fields were wet with the morning. Stillness lay over them, as if no one had passed through in a very long time.

'Where have we come from?' I asked my sister. She looked at me quizzically, half amused and half worried. Perhaps she wasn't sure whether I was playing a game.

'We've come from Barmouth,' she said.

'The caravan.'

'That's right.' That made her smile. 'That's right, the caravan.'

So these dreams I was having were repeating themselves. Each new scene was a homecoming also. Were all these reflections of some part of my head, some part of myself? Were all these stories expressions of something in me? And what did this world hold for me, what did it have to say?

'We should keep going,' my sister said, 'now that it's light.'

'All right,' I said, noting the way she held her raincoat round her. I could see that she was freezing; we had lain out in the open with nothing to shelter us, and now, in the harsh and unforgiving cold of early morning, all the heat had fled our bodies. We felt a creaking in our limbs; we felt our bloodstreams slowing. I could feel it in myself as well. I wanted to give her something to keep her warm, but realised I couldn't spare it. I was shivering myself. My feet were wet in my trainers, and my toes were freezing, and my fingers felt brittle, as if they might snap.

'Which way do we go?' I asked. She pointed along the road, out to the vast sky waking around us. A road that wound out past ploughed fields, scrubby trees and hedges, a road hand in hand with a ditch, all the way to the spot where it was drowned by the horizon. That was my fate now, to walk that way, until I was eaten up by some other story. 'We'd better get moving then,' I said. 'Best way to warm up, get the heart pumping.'

We set off walking, dragging our heavy legs along and blowing into our hands. I wondered what circumstances could ever have led to two people, two ordinary people living in England in this day and age, to spend a night sleeping under the stars in a ditch. It was as unimaginable, really, as walking all the way from Barmouth on the west coast of Wales to the cliffs above Dover. We must have been weeks, perhaps even months, on the road already. Had we passed through the Savernake Forest? I wondered. Had we walked in the shadow of Danebury hill?

Of course, there were people who travelled around as naturally as others stayed in the same place. There were Irish and Romany families living like that all over England. But this was a different story here, and I couldn't imagine its beginning. It must have begun, I supposed, in poverty, in some kind of desperation. Poverty, because the circumstances of this journey were so appalling, and desperation, because of course no one would ever choose to make such a journey on foot if they didn't have to. What horror had sent us out on to the roads like this, what tragedy? And how much longer would we have to keep trudging through this strange, half-sleeping life we were in, walking for ever, walking until we came at last to the cliffs? I wanted to ask more questions of the woman beside me, the stranger I would think of for the next little while as my sister, but knew that I mustn't. Perhaps she could overlook a few tired questions from a freezing and hungry man as he shook himself awake, explain his confusion away as a mind still clicking into the gear of morning, but that time had passed now – we were on our feet and moving. She would become suspicious of me if I still didn't know what was happening. That was the last thing I wanted.

I realised with a shock of sorrow and loneliness that this woman was the first person to have shown me any kindness since

I had walked out on my wife, left her in our flat in all my cruelty and anger. Now that cruelty had been reflected back on me so bright that it was blinding, and I didn't want to frighten the first person I'd met in all this time who'd offered something different. This was a chance to feel safer than I had done in what seemed already like a long time.

And, thinking about it, I guessed that it was a long time since I had been at home. A period that must have stretched to a fortnight, when I thought back to all the time I had spent in the bunker, the days spent waiting till I broke out and fled through the fields. The enormity of that thought made me want to howl, made me wish I could fall down and weep under the weight of it. I felt so impossibly distant from the woman I loved, so lost out here in the indifferent open country, the land staring blank and faceless at me as I walked this long grey road. I wanted to scream till she found me again, scream and bawl till she took me home and made things all right, and made things different.

It had been a proud and arrogant man who walked out on his wife that endless time ago, stubborn and overcome with the sense of his own importance. I didn't feel like that man any more. The whirlwind of my life since that time had left me humbled, and I would have given anything, said anything, if someone had only shown me how to get home. But I couldn't talk about it. Not now. Not while this woman didn't know the whole story, and suspected nothing about the stranger she was with, the man she called brother as she walked beside him on the road.

Our bodies were warmed by the blood pumping through them, and the sky grew lighter as we forged a path knifelike into the day, and after half an hour I felt a little more human. We hadn't spoken since we'd climbed out of the ditch and started walking, but I decided it was worthwhile risking a few questions.

'How much further, do you think?'

My sister pursed her lips, trying to guess at an answer.

'I think we'll probably get there this afternoon,' she said.

'As close as that?'

'I think so.' She looked around us speculatively. 'Although I suppose we can't really be sure.'

'But today we might just get there.'

'Yes.' She seemed very serious thinking of this. 'I think we will.'

'Well then.'

'So today is the day, I suppose.' She looked at me, and I was alarmed to see her face flood with compassion. What did she mean? Where were we going and what waited for us at the end of that journey?

'Yes. Today is the day.' I tried to drink in the fields all around me. This, I supposed, was Kent. We were winding our way up to what felt like high ground, way up above sea level, clean air and silence and tractors in the distance. I thought of the Downs, and guessed maybe we were crawling along the side of those till they snaked their way down to the sea again. Was that the right shape to the land around Dover? It wasn't a part of England I had seen ever so often. Still – I was seeing it now, I supposed.

'Do we have anything left to eat?' I said.

'We ate everything left last night,' my sister answered. Then she laughed again, and once again I thought of a skylark taking wing. 'I don't know what's happened to you – you're forgetful this morning.'

We heard the sea before we saw or smelled it. I learned that morning that you reach the sea sense by sense, as if it were creeping up on you. One sensation at a time the sea invades your consciousness, just in the same way it claims you as you wade in, just as it might fill the caverns of your lungs if you were pulled under and drowned. The sea invades. The first sign was the echo of the calling of gulls. Then we saw them circling in the high air over our heads, and looked at one another, and my sister smiled as if this was good news, so I smiled with her. Then we smelled salt on the air, and she smiled at me again, because we knew we were closer.

'I can almost taste it,' she said to me. I smiled, because I didn't know why we were going to where we were going. I didn't know what I was supposed to say.

'Should we stop and break?' I asked her.

She shrugged. 'Are you tired?'

'A little.' In truth I was in agony, I felt exhausted; all the sleepless trekking this body had done before my mind had been caged into it was in my ankles and my feet and knees. The weight of my body was making me limp, and I wanted to take the load off my feet for a minute. I felt weak with the hunger in me, and thought I could hear a high buzzing in my ear, like the strange deafening tinnitus that afflicts a person when they start to faint. Even if there was nothing in our bags that we could eat, it would be good to rest for a moment.

We sat down panting and dehydrated by the side of the road. My sister seemed distant and preoccupied, chewing anxiously at a lock of hair, so I didn't speak. Instead I decided to explore the contents of my bag, and see what it was that I was lugging all this way, and whether I might be able to get rid of any of it. I dragged the bag so that it rested on the ground between my legs, and unzipped the compartment. At the top I found waterproof trousers, and several pairs of socks and boxer shorts that had already been worn – of course, we were almost at the end of our journey, so it made sense that most of the contents of my bag was dirty washing. Below those items I saw a sealed bag, soft and malleable, that seemed to contain some kind of powder. I pulled it out to take a closer look, and just as I heard a sharp intake of breath from my sister, I realised that the bag was filled with ashes.

'What are you doing?' I looked up to see her glaring at me, uneasy and afraid. I stuffed the ashes back into my rucksack.

'Nothing. I just wanted to look.'

She nodded uneasily, as if she understood but didn't quite approve. I closed the rucksack again, unsettled and alarmed. I remembered the urn I had found in my hands the first time I had encountered this woman, and the urn she herself had been holding. I felt certain that there was a similar bag containing similar ashes in her rucksack as well; and somehow I felt sure without knowing why that these must be the ashes of our mother and father. I pulled myself back to my feet. I wished I could ask questions but it still felt like the wrong thing to do, to break the peace of this morning. Best to start walking again, try to outrun the alarm growing in me. I felt driven on somehow by an energy not quite my own. Best not to look too closely at what was happening – the thing to do was to keep walking on.

We started to make our way forward again, and I let my mind run away from me. Why were we here? Why were we doing this? Why was I lost in these fragmented scenes, always distant from the life I thought I ought to be living? The injustice of it stung me. Of course, everyone's life is a little like this; every door any one of us passes through is a door into a new and different world, because that's the way with the past, it's always vanishing. We were always breaking new ground, every minute, and leaving the things we'd seen behind, and we fooled ourselves if we ever thought otherwise. I knew that lots of people experienced their lives in something like the way I was experiencing this one – but not quite like this. Not as savagely, remorselessly as this. Not everyone's life felt so refracted. I couldn't understand why this should have happened to me.

We must be walking to Dover to scatter the ashes of our parents. It dawned on me – that was surely the only explanation for what was going on. Perhaps that explained why we had walked all the way as well – perhaps there was something penitential about what we were doing. People walked long distances to show their devotion on the pilgrimage of Santiago de Compostela, after all. Perhaps I had walked from Barmouth to Dover with my sister in order that we could show our devotion to our mother and father. As these thoughts occurred to me, we crested the peak of the hill, like a great slow wave passing through the lives of the people living on it, and looking ahead of us saw our first glimpse of the sea.

Before we are anything else, we are island people. Almost none of us came from this place we now call home – I suppose you could say none of us is from here at all, if you go back far enough. None of us was home here when the world began. So I think we all feel somewhere deep within us a love for the sea. It was our path when we made our way to the new life.

I think the other reason I always stop and stare at the sea is that it seems so vast, so simple and unnatural, that it's hard for my mind, which works in symbols and yarns, not to suspect that the whole thing's a dream or metaphor. How could something so big exist, after all? My instinct whenever I see the sea is to wonder what it means. The instinct is to see your own reflection in that huge mirror of the sky, and try to read the meaning of whatever you're feeling. I turned to the woman beside me and smiled.

'Here we are,' I said.

She didn't smile back, but turned to look over at the water.

'Yes,' she said. 'Today's the day then.'

Impulsively, I took her hand. I thought perhaps she wouldn't mind; we were brother and sister, after all. And something about her had become very sad and isolated as we had come closer to the coast this morning, and I wanted her to feel that she wasn't on her own.

'Don't worry,' I said. 'It'll be all right.' And she turned back and looked at me, and smiled so that her sad eyes were shining, and then we walked on, but she didn't let go of my hand. We walked hand in hand towards the place where the land disappeared, silent like children.

I thought of nothing but the pain in my feet and the hunger in my belly and the chafing at my thighs in my wet clothes as we started to be overtaken by a few more cars, and crossed a dual carriageway, and had to cross a bridge over a big road to get ever closer to the place where the land ended and gave way to the sea. People passed us, looking sideways, and I supposed that we did look strange, damp and cold and unhappy in our cheap waterproofs, holding hands like people do in happy endings. I let her lead me on and on till we saw the car park at the top of the cliffs ahead of us, a few cars parked up, a few people setting off on walks with binoculars, umbrellas, woolly hats to keep their ears cosy like eggs or teapots. We slowed for a moment, and took in the people after so long walking on our own. Then we started to walk towards the cliff.

'Are you ready?' the woman beside me said, and I guessed she wanted us to open our bags and give our parents to the wind.

'I think so, yes,' I said. 'Are you?'

'I don't think I'll ever be ready, not quite. I just don't see what else there is to do.'

We came to the edge of the land and stopped, and she kept her hand in mine. I looked down, and the vast and endless drop gave me steep-sided, frightening vertigo. I wanted to step back, but felt somehow rooted where I was. There is something in long drops that seems to make people want to fall down into them, into the arms of the absence below. I don't know the root of that longing. But death has a way of luring you in. My sister turned and looked at me.

'I love you. There might be no one else in the world any more, but I still love you.' Her words were so intense, so heavy with their meaning, that I felt a rush of love. Sometimes people just say words. Sometimes people think they mean what they're saying. And then very occasionally you hear something that strikes a note in you so deep it sets your body ringing. I loved her in that moment for the depth of her feeling, even though I didn't know her name.

Then she turned and threw herself off the cliff, and pulled me over with her.

Would I have been able to change things if I had seen what was coming? Should I have realised earlier the fate this poor woman was walking towards, and intervened, and tried to stop her from what she was doing? I ask myself that very often, now I'm old. My mind was taken up with my own troubles, and the image of the scattering of ashes, and I never thought of what the Dover cliffs were famous for. Was there something I could have done? We fell, and I screamed, and I felt my heart bursting in my chest. In the edge of my vision I saw my sister's eyes wide open, the speed of our fall distorting her face, her lips pinned back in a rictus scream. The air tried to tear my limbs away from me, snatching them back so they flailed as my body fell. I felt the ligaments of my body being torn at by the fall as the blood rushed through me, and I lost my vision as the sound of the sea drowned my ears and the world went black.

But of course, my story didn't end there. I passed into a different world, just as I had done when I'd fallen into the river. And still I was not allowed to rest.

My eyes snapped open once again, and I found myself gasping, dragging air into my lungs, panicked and afraid, as if I had woken from a dream. Except that I knew it hadn't been a dream – it had been two people dying, it had been me dying. I had woken into some new place – some kind of police or prison cell, I saw as I glanced around me. Back in the unrecoverable lost world of my past, I was dead, and the woman who called herself my sister was dead, and she had killed me, she must have killed me because she loved me. Why had she wanted to throw us both off? What could have happened that made us both want to die? And then I remembered the last thing she said to me, and the ashes in our backpacks, the urns in our hands, and I thought it must have been because we were alone. We must have decided to die together because our parents had died, and somehow we had come to the conclusion that after that, there was nothing left for us. I thought back to the caravan I had first met that woman in, the two single beds side by side, our cheap clothes, the desolate empty feeling of stepping out of that caravan and seeing the clouds over Barmouth. We must have been poor, and out of hope, and out of love. We must have decided to finish our stories by doing something grand, to wrap up our lives with a journey worth remembering. And it was remarkable somehow, to walk so far then kill yourself. Under the layers of sadness, the sense of something terrible happening, was the walk, at least, some kind of gesture of contempt, a demand that people should have listened? How many lives, I wondered, were lived like that, under low roofs, without any light getting in and shining on them, without acclaim or aspiration? Was there something brave in turning your back on living that life, just as there was something sad and pathetic in falling to your death instead?

And where had I been flung to now? I looked around me and wondered what life I might be in. I was alone in some kind of cell, wearing a stiff nylon suit that rustled loudly when my arms moved. A cheap suit, a door with a grille in the middle. My body felt frail and empty, and I felt cold, felt the bones of my knees pressed against each other. My hands in my lap looked like the hands of a stranger. I supposed I must be waiting to go into court. I supposed I was going to be put on trial now for the murders of those young women, the murders they thought I had committed. Perhaps they had found those clothes in the places I said they might have been buried. Perhaps they had been too late to save the last victim.

I leaned back against the wall of the cell, and took deep breaths, and tried to blink away the feeling of that fall I had just been hurled from, the white panic of that fainting, the despair that had dragged me over the edge of that cliff. That was the thing that scared me most. The memory of the look in that woman's eyes, my sister, the love in her eyes and the simple, naked passion, like staring at a light bulb, like electricity. So much love it had killed her. So much love that no one had wanted, all of it gone to waste, thrown over the cliff edge. I sat and lived with the memory of that woman for a little while – I don't know how long, I only know I couldn't blink it away. Then I heard the door of the room opening. I had expected a man in a prison guard's uniform, but instead I saw quite an elderly woman, accompanied by a younger woman who looked Vietnamese. The older woman started speaking, and the younger woman translated what she was saying, and I found to my surprise that I understood both of them.

'Hello, love. I'm Ethel and I'm from Witness Liaison. Annie who watched your evidence video back with you has had to go home – it was the end of her shift, so I'm taking over for this afternoon. You remember Emily, of course, who's translating for you. We're due to go up so you can give your evidence in a minute, is that all right?'

I nodded, saying nothing. So I had guessed the scene wrong – I was the boy from the bunker again, and I must have outrun my pursuers after I fell into the river, and they must have been caught, and somehow the police must have picked me up and listened.

'So like I said, we'll have a curtain up so you can't see the accused while you're giving your evidence; you'll just have the judge and the lawyers to talk to. You're allowed to take time and you're allowed to ask for breaks, you understand?'

I nodded again.

'Like your lawyer said this morning, it will be hostile, some of that questioning, but you don't have to worry. No one thinks you've done anything wrong. You're here to talk about what it was like being a victim, and if you stick to what you know and what you've said already, you'll be fine. And it's nowhere near as bad as they make it look on the television. Now, do you want to go to the toilet before we go upstairs to the courtroom?'

I shook my head. Ethel smiled and made a movement towards the door, as if it was time for us to go.

'All right then. Shall we go on up?' I followed her out into the hallway and looked around me, blinking. The place was nearly deserted, except for two security guards who were sitting at the mouth of the entrance hall, flanked by a pair of metal detector gates – one, I guessed, for going in and one for coming out. There was a TV screen screwed to the wall behind them, displaying the names of the people on trial in the different courtrooms of this building. The place seemed calm and civilised and recently disinfected. Ethel cleared her throat and I looked back at her.

'What we'll do is go up the back stairs and through the judge's landing to the witness room, I think. They suggested that might be safest.' I nodded. I didn't feel like speaking. I guessed that if I did, Ethel wouldn't have understood me. There must have been a translator waiting in the courtroom we were headed for already, waiting to make sense of all I said. Ethel led me through a glass door into a plain, anonymous concrete stairwell, and we spiralled up for two floors till I saw a bright blue carpet ahead of me in the hall. 'This is the top floor, you see,' Ethel said, leading me out into the blue, wide open space of the private hallway where the judges checked their files and robed and disrobed and had their lunch. I wondered whether every witness was led through here – it wasn't really worth having a private space for the judges, it seemed to me, if everyone who came to talk to them walked through it. We crossed the carpet and walked into another anonymous hallway, another magnolia scene, and then we were through a door and I took in cheap prints that had been framed and put up on the walls of this last room – the late Matisse, the Van Gogh sunflower, the photo of the sea, the images you see in every doctor's waiting room – and Ethel was sitting me down on a comfortable chair, and I supposed this must have been the witness room she had said we were aiming for. Out into the blue and the wide open space.

'It won't be very long now. Someone will come in and see you before they start as well. Remember – wait for the translator to finish what they're saying, and you're allowed to take as many breaks as you like. All you have to do is ask for one and the judge will say yes.'

I felt nervous, even though this wasn't really my crisis, my trial, my evidence to give. Out into the blue and the wide open space. I wondered how I'd be able to answer the questions. I only knew part of this story I was in; I couldn't tell all of it. How nerve-wracking it must be, I thought, to have to sit here waiting, not knowing what was out there for you, what was going to be said, what everyone would know already and what everyone would discover. The sense of theatre and ritual set me on edge, but for most people who came into this room I supposed there would be something more, something urgent – the knowledge that their life was about to be cut open and pinned out on display, like they were something caught by the butcherbird.

Another woman, about fifty, hair dyed blonde, came into the room and smiled at me and talked to Ethel, but I didn't really listen. I didn't know what I was going to say if I had to take the stand, I didn't know how to cover up the fact that I wasn't who they thought I was. But I didn't feel too anxious. Something told me the scene was going to change before it came to that – that was how it had worked for almost as long as I remembered now; I had been snatched away just before the moment of the crisis, and sent hurtling into another life. I realised as I thought about it that I was very tired. I hadn't slept, it seemed, since I had escaped from the underground bunker; even though I had woken in that ditch in Kent I hadn't felt the benefit of sleeping. It felt as if days had passed since then. More than that though, what I was feeling was a deeper exhaustion, a pilot light flickering inside me that seemed to want to go out. As I sat leaning my elbows on my knees and blocking out the drone of the two women's voices, I felt as if the hope was going out of me a little, as if the sense

I had clung to since things had gone wrong – that there was still a home out there for me to get back to – was growing harder to remember. How could I have any real confidence in that? How could I keep thinking there was a real life that I would be able to get back to? Didn't this moment I was in now seem as real to me as my old life had ever done? Perhaps I was just living out some cruel, extreme example of the way that everyone lived. Was I any less mired in the world right now, after all, than I had felt when I was a young man who had never imagined this? Was everyone's life just a series of new scenes they walked into that they had never visited before, and then never visited again? I couldn't tell, any more, whether this might not be the way it had always been. Maybe the world was full of people experiencing life this way. Maybe we all felt a little like this.

But how could that be the case if my wife wasn't here with me to see it? We had promised to be there for each other; how could I have lost her like this? There had to be something wrong, but I couldn't hope to find a way to fix it with the same kind of anger I'd felt before. Too much had happened in the intervening time, and the shine had worn off me, the energy seeping away. The world was too deep and dark and I didn't know how to navigate my way out of it.

You remember I told you when I started my story the reason I walked out of that fight with my wife? She showed me all of a sudden that I was only in love with myself and not with anyone else, not with her, and I couldn't handle it. Ran away from it. Well, I tell you, I sat in that court and I knew things had changed, because what I'd been through was a humbling. And all the shit I'd ever fed my head with was lost in that wood in the dark, in that bunker, on that hilltop, falling off that cliff, and I saw how lucky I'd been long ago and once upon time; I saw the miracle that had been given to me. Someone else had been sharing their life with me. I had been so lucky; I'd had everything that made life big already. And I realised then that all I'd ever wanted was my wife, who trusted me enough to share her life with me.

'All right then, love?' I had been so lucky. Ethel was looking down at me. 'Are you ready to go on?' I stood, and straightened the shirt and the tie I was wearing, and nodded to her. The woman with the bleached hair opened the door to the court-room, then stood aside to let me through. I knew already what was going to happen. I looked around me at the bad 1990s prints, and silently said goodbye. Then I walked forward, through the door to the courtroom, and that world, too, had ended.

So it went on. It gets harder to remember it all so clearly after that. Terrible to say, isn't it, but you get used to anything in the end. After I left that court, I found myself in a waiting room on a row of plastic chairs, one other man sitting there with me, further down the row, going over a script, his lips moving as he read. Almost as if I had woken back in my own life. The light of late afternoon was coming in through a window opposite, so that I had to squint a little, and the sun caught him in bars, split him into passages of light and dark as he sat there. I supposed it did the same to me. There was a script in my hands as well – I glanced at it momentarily, but I didn't feel able to take in what it said. I looked back at the other man and wondered how to talk to him. It seemed very difficult to talk to anyone now, in case I made a mistake, gave away the fact that I didn't know what I was doing. I felt very isolated, sitting there. The man must have felt I was watching him, because he looked up and caught my eye, smiled nervously.

'You been in for these guys before?' he asked.

'I don't think so.'

'I don't think they know what they want.'

'No?'

'This is my second time in. I'm reading for a different part. I think they're just hoping the right actor walks through the door.'

'Some people are like that, aren't they?'

'Don't know what they want?'

'Yeah, maybe.'

'Have you had any work recently?' the man asked me.

I tried to think back.

'Not so recently.'

He shook his head.

'Me neither. Not much this time of year.'

I wondered at this.

'Maybe not.'

'Don't you think?'

'Well, I think it might just be you and me are on a bad run. We might just be having bad luck.'

'Yeah?'

'I've heard actors almost every month of the year tell me there's never really anything out there that month. I think there's always work, we just come in and out of focus, all of us.'

The other actor considered this. I suppose he thought I was being chippy. I found it hard to keep my focus entirely on what I'd said – it was hard to commit to this one conversation when I knew there was so much more going on above our heads, other stories abandoned halfway through, other lives waiting.

'I suppose so, yeah.'

A woman came into the room then, and made eye contact with me, and smiled.

'Hi, we're ready for you.' I stood, and nodded to the other man as I walked past him. The scene felt so familiar to me as I stepped out of it, and I wondered whether it might perhaps have been my life – but as I walked into the audition room, the world changed once more.

I found myself swimming, in what looked like the Hampstead ponds. There were one or two other people in the water with me, and I was doing breaststroke along the shallow edge of the water. There were people walking through a park all round us. I could feel the sun on my shoulders, the delicious cool of the water around me, holding me, like a forgetting. I ducked my head under the surface, and that world, too, had ended.

I found myself at a dining table on a patio under a sky filled up with summer. A family sat around me speaking Spanish in loud and happy voices. There was a ladle in my hand. I took in the people who were sitting with me. A woman in her early thirties, a girl who looked about seven or eight, two boys who were younger, an elderly woman bent low over the plate in front of her, unable to take in very much of life. When they spoke I knew what they were saying.

'Have you washed your hands?' the younger woman said to the three children, as they shifted on their chairs and swung their legs.

'Yes,' said the older of the two boys.

'All of you?'

This time the girl answered.

'We all have.'

The woman looked to me, smiling, relaxed, not thinking that I was anyone but who she assumed me to be.

'Do you want to serve?'

I filled the plates of the children and the two women with paella from an earthenware dish in the middle of the table, and started to join in the conversation, and found that I spoke Spanish too.

'This looks good,' I said.

The woman smiled.

'Thank you.'

I looked to the children as I ladled rice on to their plates.

'You three are lucky.'

I imagined these people were my family – they all seemed to know me, all seemed to be my friends. As long as I stuck to this idea, it seemed to be possible to navigate the conversation. I couldn't tell whether I was a father or even a grandfather in this scene, except that I saw my hands were not the hands of a young man; they were worn by work, the veins standing out under my skin. I ran a hand through my hair and the hair on the top of my head felt thin, and I wondered who that made me, what age I was, what role I was playing at this table. Then one of the children called me 'Dad'. I held forth as best I could, and talked about a day at work in an office, tedious office politics, making it all up off the top of my head but knowing no one would notice, because the terrible thing about offices is that they're all the same; everyone has the same intrigues and arguments the whole world over.

'Half the morning I wasted on a paper jam.'

'Oh, that's terrible,' the woman who I guessed must be my wife replied.

'So frustrating. You ask someone to fix it but it goes on and on. In the end I joined in, but I don't know what I'm doing, no one ever really knows how to work the photocopier.'

'I know. Did you like your lunch?'

'Fantastic.'

She smiled.

It wasn't clear to me whether my wife spent her days making my lunch and making my dinner, or if she too went to work, so I tried to be careful and discover as much as I could.

'How was your day?' I asked.

She shrugged.

'Oh, fine. I have a lot of marking to do.'

A teacher. I felt relief – in my experience, teaching is another job with the same pressures and frustrations wherever you go around the world. It's another conversation you can bluff your way through without too much trouble.

'I'm sorry.'

'It's OK.'

'How long till term ends now?'

The woman gave me a quizzical look.

'What do you mean? It's only just started.'

'I know!' I said, desperately covering. 'I just wish it was over again.'

She laughed at that, and I seemed to have got away with it.

'When term ends again we'll go away on holiday,' said the girl to my right.

I turned to her, smiling.

'Yes, we will. And where will we go?'

The girl leapt from her chair in excitement.

'Disneyland!' I turned to my wife to see whether this idea met with parental approval. She smiled and rolled her eyes.

'Maybe.'

The girl seemed insistent.

'You promised, Dad, you promised.'

'Did I?' I asked. My wife came to my rescue, never suspecting how uncertain I really was of whether I had promised any such thing.

'We said we would think about it, didn't we? And we will think about it. If you work hard at school and do well, and if we can afford to go on the trip, then we'll go on the trip.'

'I don't want to share a room,' said the older boy.

'We might all have to share a room, who knows,' I said.

At this moment, the elderly woman at the other end of the table seemed to tut, and pushed her plate away from her. My wife noticed as well.

'Are you OK, Mama?' she asked.

The old woman turned to look at us both.

'You spoil them, you know that?'

'Do we?' I could sense my wife becoming tense, becoming defensive. Perhaps this was a regular argument, and she didn't want to have it once again.

'You spoil them all the time.'

'I think a family can go on a holiday, can't they?' my wife said.

'Maybe they can. I never went on any holiday, but what do I know?'

'Perhaps it would have been good if we had.'

This incensed the woman – my mother-in-law – and she turned in her seat to face her daughter.

'So now you're saying we never did anything for you, is that it?'

'No, Mama, that's not what I'm saying. Don't start an argument. We're trying to enjoy our dinner.'

The old lady tutted again.

'Sure we are. And very good it is too.'

My wife clearly sensed some hidden meaning in this.

'Thank you,' she said, guarded and watching carefully to see what was coming next.

'As well it should be, seeing as it's my recipe.'

I decided I ought to try and join in myself.

'And a very good recipe it is,' I said, 'and very well cooked.'

My mother-in-law shook her head and picked up her fork, and went back to eating her dinner.

At the end of the meal I told my children to wash up the dishes, and got up from the table with my wife. Her mother stood as well, and went inside, saying nothing. She shuffled, and it was clear from the way she walked that she had bad arthritis in her legs. We headed towards the lawn.

'You find her frustrating,' I said.

My wife laughed, though she hadn't found me funny.

'You know I do,' she said.

'You handle her well.'

'I just feel so sad to see her the way she is. Old, and closing up, and becoming bitter at the thought of life. She didn't use to be like that.'

'People change as they grow older.'

'I wish I could show her there are good things still to come.'

'Time with her grandchildren.'

'Exactly.' She turned to me in agreement, looked me in my eyes. 'But she spends no time with the children. It is sad that Father died, but it's not a reason to give up on everything.'

So she was widowed. Perhaps that had been when she had moved into this house with us; when she was suddenly on her own, and shaken by grief, and my wife was feeling guilty about her mother rattling round the house she had shared with her father.

'It might just take time before she feels able to be happy again. Before she feels she is allowed to be that way, maybe.'

The woman bent forwards to smell a yellow rose that was climbing up the wall at the side of the house.

'I don't know, maybe. I wish she would hurry up though. It is hard to work hard and feel at the end of every day as if you ought to be apologising for something. When you don't ever know what you've done.'

'Well, that's easy,' I said.

She turned to me, surprised.

'Is it?'

'Yes. You're still here, and your father isn't. That is difficult for her. You are a reminder. She wouldn't put it like that herself, I'm sure, but it's hard for her to see you and think back to when you were young.'

The woman took a moment to consider this.

'Yes,' she said in the end. 'It's hard always to think back to when you were young, isn't it? And remember when things were different. And all the more painful when you're grieving.' She laughed then.

'What's funny?' I asked her.

'I was just thinking of church music,' she said. 'When I was little I used to sing, "in the midst of life, we are in death," and I didn't know what the words meant, not really. And then you get all this way through life, years and years later, and you never sing with anyone any more, and the words finally become useful. You finally see what they mean. Isn't that lovely? A little lesson buried in our memories for when we are ready to learn it.'

So it went on. A lifetime like this. I found myself in Nepal's main airport, as the building was shelled by the Nepalese army to quell a revolution; I found myself imprisoned in the Maldives, being spirited from one jail to another by speedboat so that human rights organisations didn't know where I was; I found myself on stage playing Edgar in a production of *King Lear*, and felt my heart almost stop as I spoke the words, 'Who is't can say "I am at the worst"? The worst is not so long as we can say "This is the worst."' And I watched Gloucester, my father, make his way on to the stage, eyes bandaged where they had been torn out, seeking for the Dover cliffs to throw himself from them into the sleep and forgiveness of oblivion, and I realised with a cold clarity that I had been to that place myself – I had done that, thrown myself from those cliffs, felt the wind tear at me like a judgement. And I watched Gloucester as he staggered on to stage, leaning on an old stick, and felt just like him. I felt someone had taken my eyes.

From time to time I thought I caught glimpses of my wife. In another country, I knelt in shock and horror when someone showed me a statue of her. Then even as I watched, the stone seemed to melt, and she to move, and begin to move towards me – but I swooned away, fainted at the fright of what had happened, and when I woke she was gone. I was in a different world, mopping a school gymnasium with dirty water, listening to the echoes of my movements bounce off the hall. Once I even found myself back on the estate where I had lived with her, and ran in frightened recognition to the building that had been our home. But as I ran I crossed a road, and didn't look where I was going. A van hit me and when I woke, I was in another world. Things conspired to keep me from my old life, and I only had moments like these, little glimpses.

Occasionally, I saw other people I had known before things went wrong. I remember sitting in the front row of a funeral, sombre in a dark suit, and wondering where I was, then looking down at the programme to realise all of a sudden that it was my mother in the coffin; I was present at my mother's burial. Once, sitting in the cheap seats at Lord's for a test match, I thought I saw my father on the other side of the stadium. There was even a night when, quite inexplicably, I found myself drinking with an old friend from school. That was perhaps the strangest scene I ever played out, because it was so eerily like coming home.

He knew my name, and talked as if there was nothing wrong with me, as if I hadn't vanished.

'The thing is, though, the trouble is that people thought totally differently when we were growing up, didn't they? It's not that we thought the same stuff you read now and just didn't bother with it – being young when we were young was a whole different head space, wasn't it?'

'Sure.' I played along.

'I mean, I didn't use to leave the heating on all winter because I didn't care about climate change, did I? I left it on cos I left it on – I didn't think about climate change.'

'Right.'

'And I should have. I can see that now, can't I? But no one taught me to then, did they, because the world wasn't the world it is now.'

'Yeah.'

'This is what no one understands. You can't judge someone whose life you haven't lived. You can't judge anyone, not in the end, not really. Because you never know where they're coming from, what standards they're holding themselves to. I've had to totally re-educate myself about so many things over the years. Not because I think I was prejudiced. Not because I thought I was some dickhead. Just because I was brought up one way and now that's not the way the world sees things any more, so I have to shift into line. I mean, it used to be a good thing to hold doors open for women, didn't it? And now that's offensive to some people.'

'Is it?'

'Some women get offended if you hold open doors, for sure. I mean, I think it's all right still really, I think it's polite, but I know people pass comments. And then I've had to learn about gay people being OK. You remember, when we were growing up, there was no one telling us it was OK to be gay. And being honest, that took some getting my head round, because you get used to one way of thinking, don't you, you get stuck into one thing. But now I've got used to having been wrong, I can see I was wrong. Cos it was always wrong to have a go at someone cos of their skin, wasn't it, that was never all right.'

'No.'

'And being gay, it's not that different. It's who someone is. Like someone's skin. You have to get over it, that's all, don't you?'

'Right.'

'I think the problem with the people who brought us up, our parents' generation, and I guess all the generations before them, I think they were really frightened. Because you couldn't travel so much or so far, could you, even forty years ago. So no one had seen that much of the world. And there was this sort of – this fear of the world, anything that wasn't like you. But that's changed now, we're getting over that. Because we've seen more of difference.'

'Sure, yeah.'

'Anyway. You think Palace are going down this season?'

We drained six pints together, talking about old times, talking about careers and marriages and deaths and children – he seemed to know that I'd never had any children – and then when the barman called time we walked out of the pub together, and I never saw him again, because once more the world changed around me and so my friend had vanished. I felt bereft that night, when I found a place to sleep beneath an orange tree in what I thought might be the south of Italy. For a moment I had almost dared to believe I was coming home, and the pain was always sharpest when I let hope in.

Sometimes I was flung back into the past. I remember waking to the siege of Basingstoke in the early days of the English Civil War, sitting among other soldiers outside the fortifications of Basing House, watching the cannons fire on the walls and knowing we'd never get through them, not only because of the size of the fortress before us, but also because I knew how things went in the history books. And I was there, as well, when Owain Glyndwr starved the English out of Harlech Castle – I was among the twenty men who eventually surrendered and walked, emaciated and defeated, out of the keep to let him take up residence in what became the heart of his brief kingdom.

It started with a terrible hunger. A dizziness, and a gnawing pain, and a weakness in the legs. I was standing in the lee of a huge stone wall, sheltered from the rain, looking up to the battlements, another man beside me. His face was pinched and sunken, his skin a bluish pale, and I knew as I looked at him that I must look the same, because he had the outward symptoms of everything I was feeling. The man watched me steadily.

'Is it today?' he asked me. I said nothing. I didn't know what to say. But that was answer enough for him, it seemed; he nodded and began to move. 'Walk with me,' he said.

I followed him up a set of winding stone steps, out to the perilous and narrow walkway at the top of the castle's battlements, and it was here that I realised I was in Harlech. I looked out to the sea beyond us, and felt sure I had stood in this place before. Today, the sea is a mile further out than it was in Glyndwr's time, and there is a golf course in the place where now I saw waves crashing and dying beneath me; but I knew I had been here all the same, on a childhood holiday long ago, and stood in this place and tried to see into the distance, and not been certain what it was I was seeing. I stood next to the other man in silence, and we watched the waves crash and fall.

'It should not have happened like this,' he said. 'It should not have been possible for one Welsh prince to face down England. And we will be damned for it. We will be forever shamed. He has faced down the strength of Harlech, and we should have been enough to see him back. How has it happened? How has it happened like this?'

Still, I said nothing. I didn't feel I had the right to, somehow. I had not lived through what this man seemed to have lived through, though I shared the hunger now; for as long as I stood with him I was sharing the pain. He carried on speaking.

'The curse is that we will be forgotten,' he said. 'I thought that was what would happen to Glyndwr. A landowner's rebellion, quickly dismissed, quickly seeming like it never even happened. And England going on and on. But that's not what's happened. Here we are, and we have been defeated – we have become part of his story now, not of our own.'

'What do you mean?' I asked.

He turned and shrugged at me.

'No one will ever talk about the men who kept Harlech Castle any more. Harlech will just be a place Glyndwr once claimed. We will be damned in our lifetime, and after we have died we will all be forgotten. The rules of war are merciless. There has to be a winner and there has to be a loser, and the loser gets nothing at all.' He turned and looked back out to sea. I stood with him, saying nothing, taking in the grey sky and feeling the wind buffet against us. After a while he turned and started walking back down towards the castle keep.

'Come,' he said. 'I will tell the others.'

'You're sure today's the day?' I asked.

He didn't even answer. We walked into a darkened room where men sat round with their heads in their hands, their legs balled up to their chests, no fire stuttering, because I guessed if we were all this starved, then the wood supply had run out long ago as well. The man I was following stood in the middle of the room and looked at the huddled forms around him.

'It's time,' he said. Then he left, and I didn't follow him. I stayed among the half-dead men, the grey, tired men huddled together for warmth in the dark stinking room, and wondered what was going to happen. After half an hour, the man I had gone up to the battlements with came back in.

'They're ready,' he said. 'They have accepted our surrender. We must come out so that they can come in.'

'What will happen to us then?' asked a man seated against the wall furthest from the door.

'Who knows? Perhaps we will be kept here as prisoners. Or perhaps we will be let loose to travel away from here, find some shelter, spread the news that Glyndwr has Harlech now.'

No one said anything then. The man who seemed to be our leader left the room again, and then one by one everyone stood and walked out to stand behind the castle gate, kicking their heels, pale and waiting. I counted the heads in front of me. Twenty men were stood around, twenty poor souls who would be dead and nameless and forgotten almost before you could take in the fact of their existence. The world moves so quick; it eats people up so quick. The leader gave a signal and two of the men moved to open the gate, and as it rose we saw the Welsh soldiers waiting in silence for us. Nothing showing on their faces, only the stone faces of hard men who had starved twenty soldiers out of a castle they could not take by force. Just sheer iron will waiting for us beyond the gate. We walked out to meet them. And I remember as I passed through the gate the world changed again, and I found myself lying in a hospital bed, a spotless modern hospital, and I shook, and saw things all round the room that couldn't have been there, bright colours like ghosts that couldn't have been there. And one of the ghosts bent down over me, and then a stethoscope came out of the air and I felt it cold against my chest, and my consciousness vanished. I think perhaps that was one of the times that I've died; I think in that moment I was a man in a hospital with delirium tremens, which kills more people than you'd know, with the lights dancing in front of my eyes like the light through branches, like a dancing tree.

I found myself crouched in the bottom of a trench, wet sucking mud around my boots, my feet rotten and the stink coming off them turning my stomach. I could feel the way the flesh was stretching away from the bone, ruined and coming apart like old thread. I could feel a hunger in my body, a weakness, as if I hadn't eaten in days. I looked around and saw men in a long line either side of me in the distinctive uniforms of the British army during the First World War. The young man next to me – he wasn't really much more than a boy – looked pale with fear.

'I feel like I'll be sick,' he said.

'You're all right,' I told him, not knowing what else to say, not knowing what battle we were about to walk into. 'Not long now.'

'That's the trouble,' he replied, and smiled in spite of himself. I felt my thighs cramping from the way we crouched against the wet mud of the side of the trench, the ladder reaching up above us to the surface and to death. I wondered how long we had been here, crouched like this.

'My legs are seizing up,' I said.

The boy nodded. Then a thought seemed to strike him.

'Do you think there's likely to be a God, then?' he asked me.

I wondered what to say.

'Why do you ask?'

'Well, I suppose I've never known, really. Always sung the hymns and put the cassock on and got on with it, and never thought. But thinking seriously, I never seriously believed. Only in the ritual.' He thought about this for a moment. 'I'd like there to be a God today, though,' he said.

'Why?'

'Because if He existed, I think I'd get a feeling in advance that I was going to die. You know, I think you'd feel it coming. And I don't have any feeling – it just feels like another morning, and hunger, and fear. So either that means there isn't a God . . . or on the other hand it means I might survive.'

He had no chance to offer any more; a whistle blew along the line, and another young man who looked barely more than a boy, wearing an officer's uniform, fixed his eyes on us and placed his hands on the ladder.

'All right, men,' he said, his voice quavering. 'Up the ladder, and then when we get to the top we form ranks. Then we march, no running, till we reach the other side, all right?' My heart sank. Perhaps we were at the Somme, perhaps some other battle, but I knew what this had led to every time it was tried in the First World War; thousands of the men around me now were going to die. As this reality sank in, the officer took hold of the ladder and levered himself up out of the trench. The boy who hoped there was a God followed after him, and then it was my turn. I reached the surface and already I could hear bullets like wasps shrilling ahead of us, see the mud fly where they bit the ground. We formed into a line. I felt hollow, so full of grief for these men around me who were going to die. The officer's face was white with fear, but he looked along the line, waved back one man who was advancing too quickly.

'In line now, stay in line!' We walked forwards, and the light of early morning on the ground lit up in stark relief the places where the earth had been churned and roiled with this war's violence, the blood and soil slicked together into a new thing, like a new element, like you could pick up death and hold it in your hands. I heard and felt a sudden thud to my right, and turned, and saw that the stock of my rifle had disappeared, shot clean away. The bullets from the opposite trench had found our range, and were reaching us. I heard another impact to my left, and turned to see. The boy I had been speaking to fell forwards, his head shot clean away. The officer kept looking along the line, shouting to us to close up, keep going, hold the line. And I marched. I did not turn and flee. I marched forwards because that was what so many had done before me, and it seemed the only way to do right by them – not turn and run, no matter the madness I was caught in. We saw the opposite trench. More of us died, but we kept going. We reached the barbed wire and forced a way through, and started firing. We checked our bayonets as we marched. We reached the mouth of the other trench, and descended into hell.

I slipped across the world, through time, until a sense of vertigo overwhelmed me, until I could hardly engage with anything. You couldn't imagine how many lives I've lived, how many different worlds I've woken to. And I wish that had made life richer for me, but the truth is it hasn't worked like that. What I've felt ever since this started is that I've become a stone, heavy and dead like a stone, and the world is a river I'm skimming over and can't enter into. I can't seem to be a part of life; I can only glimpse life, glance through it and grasp moments, grasp nothing of any real weight. And it makes me feel as if I'm dead. I feel as if the whole world is only memories happening to me, or dreams, and that my real body isn't this one I'm in, my real body is somewhere else, lying somewhere else, deep down in some casket and unspooling all these memories till it is empty of stories.

When I feel close to people, or feel love from people, those are the cruellest times of all. I have woken in beds beside strange women, or women who seemed somehow familiar to me, and seen love in their eyes, and not even known their names, and it breaks my heart every time it happens, because it only makes me feel further from the dream of the woman I once loved, the woman I abandoned. I have sung in pubs and on terraces with other men, drunk beer, felt camaraderie, then walked away from the scene and never seen any of those people ever again. I have sat with children on my lap and known they were supposed to be mine, and seen the vulnerability in them, and the life, and the love they had and the need to be loved, and felt nothing, no connection, and felt like I was betraying them as I let them climb over me as if I were the limbs of some dead tree. In the midst of sex, I've felt overwhelmed by the absurdity of this life, my ghost life, and not been able to look the person I'm with in the eyes. In the midst of life I have felt dead.

And always, like a chorus coming back round again, there has been the abiding refrain of time spent waiting. I've noticed that, more than anything else, these dreams I've poured through have often been preoccupied with that. That is like so many other lives, of course, so many ordinary lives; we all spend so long in the waiting rooms of surgeries, in queues for lunch, on hold, in anticipation. Life is anticipation for very many people, though of what I'm never sure. But people always look to me as if they're waiting – that's how people put up with things, I think. The indignities that wear them. I have found myself time and again on plastic bucket seats outside a room, alongside others who look like me, alongside men and women staring at their hands until a young person staring at a clipboard comes into the room and calls their name, and releases them from the purgatory of the plastic chair. So many times I've stood upon hearing my own name and felt relief, without even knowing what I had been relieved from. And without having been released at all from the purgatory at the centre of my life – this wandering, this endless alienation from any kind of story that could link up the scenes of my life into sense. That has never let me go; I'm waiting for the end to that feeling still.

This was what my life became, after the night when I lost the thread of it. So it went on. The same thing kept happening again and again – I experienced my life not as a single river that was flowing through me, but as different streams that I hopped between, one brief breath of life after another, and never the whole thing, never the real thing. Some lives I visited for only a moment, some would recur like theme tunes, some would last for seconds and others for weeks. I never saw any of it coming. It went on like this for thirty years or more, one strange story after another, like the shapes a fire throws over the wall, always repeating, always changing, like the images you see in a kaleidoscope, endlessly varying, one alien image following another. This strange, seasick feeling of having lost the thread became my life, and even now, all this time later, it is still the life I am in. Just half an hour ago, before I walked into this bar, I was in an entirely different world to this one. If you rewound my life now, and played it backwards and watched it happening, you'd see me spit this drink back out, then stand and walk with my head turned away from the light out of these doors, and straight into a garden shed somewhere in some rainy city. That was where I was before I met you. Wearing layers and layers of jumpers like someone used to being outside in bad weather. I woke from sleep, and found myself curled up in a shed in somebody's back garden. There was a window in the shed, and I looked out, and saw a pylon looming in the distance on the top of a hill. I sat for a bit, feeling tired, feeling groggy, and feeling the ache in my knees because my legs were curled up under me and I had gone stiff in the cold out there. I listened to the sound of rain on the roof of the shed, my favourite sound for as far back as I can remember, one of the few places I ever find in the world these days where I feel a little safe, in fact. I can listen to rain falling on a roof above me and no matter where I am, it takes me back to memories of childhood, hiding in greenhouses listening to rain, or even further back, being pushed along in a pram with a waterproof cover over me and the rain drumming gently. I love that safe feeling. I think it reminds me of feeling loved. It has been a long time since I felt that way about anyone, or anyone felt that way about me. It's not that I ever stopped loving my wife – but it has been decades since we parted. I suppose she wouldn't recognise me now.

That was the hardest thing about the years as they passed, I think. After a while – it's strange what you get used to – I found I didn't mind so much about never knowing quite what life I was about to find myself in. It even had its advantages. I never seemed to have to earn any money, or pay any bills; I parachuted in and out of lives where that was already happening, so a lot of the drudgery of life seemed to fade away for me. And maybe it sounds like clutching at straws, but I do think that's some kind of privilege. Only to have to live moments in a life, the moments that seem to lift you up out of things. Never to really have to do the washing up, the bits in between. The world has spun round, and as of this moment, I'm still clinging on to it, and I think that's been a privilege, no matter how strange or unusual my story may seem. But the thing that has never quite got any better has been that sensation of missing my wife.

For the first few years after it happened, I lost a lot of sleep; I used to break down quite regularly. I tried to dream up ways of finding her again. Hitchhiking my way to the flat we had moved into when the whole thing started, or calling her number, or writing a letter. But my plans never worked for some reason. The scene always changed before the call went through, before I got to the right city, before I managed to buy a stamp. Fate wanted us apart, and I never outwitted it. After the first few years, I started to come to terms with that reality. I saw very clearly, once she was gone, that she had always been everything to me: my whole life, my meaning. I had just been young, I'd been naive, hadn't understood the course my life was taking. It hadn't even struck me yet that life evolves its patterns and we all fall in with them – I still thought, when I was twenty-five, that I could be anyone. And do anything.

She taught me so much, after I lost her, and I mourned that very keenly, because I wished I had been old enough when we had been together that I could have slowed down my life and given more time to her, and listened. But these are the mistakes we all make when we're young, I suppose. And we all lose time we might have spent with loved ones, because of our ambition. I have perhaps lived out the costs of that in a more extreme way than other people. It's a strange thought to conjure with. For a very long time, I confess, I thought I had been cursed. But more and more these days, as I grow older, as I think back over the worlds I've seen, I start to wonder whether it wasn't a blessing.

The memories I have, I burnish and cherish them. Like a stone that I keep in my pocket, running my thumb over its surface all day long. I love them very dearly. And spending all these years going over and over them has made me feel very lucky. Because maybe I didn't get as much time with my wife as I would have wanted, but I did meet her. I did get the years we spent together. I do have this much, and that's not nothing. Because she was an extraordinary woman, the woman I married. She was very alive, and very fragile, and very beautiful, and I count myself very lucky to have known her and been close to her, even for a moment. And perhaps if I had lived differently, I wouldn't see quite so clearly on that front. Our lights might have gone out till we couldn't feel anything. She'll have been all right again in the end, I think. She'll have given up on me, and gone on with her life. And that will have hurt her, and I wish it didn't happen, but it did, so I have to hope she moved on from me and found happiness again.

I'm sorry, I've talked for so long, haven't I? I've talked for so long. I never tell this story. I never think anyone will listen, let alone believe me. You know how it is. A man of a certain age on his own. People tend to keep their distance. Then the minute you open your mouth to tell them something like this, they're convinced that you're mad, so they get up and move away sharpish before you stab them, or I don't know what. I'm sorry. Sometimes you meet someone and it feels as if there's life to be lived between you, do you ever find that? There are things to be said, and things that need hearing. I don't know whether that's really true, but it's something I've learned to look out for over the years. The way I live, most people fly past you – you barely even see them. It's impossible for any of them to matter to you. But every now and then I've met people who seem to be like magnets. Like flames. As if they might slow me down on this whirlpool journey I'm spiralling in, and I've always tried to talk to them, on the occasions when they cross my path. Sometimes they've helped me stay in one place for a little bit. And I like doing that, just taking a breather. It helps me to take stock and work out where I am.

Three

Let him that was the cause of this have power
To take off so much grief from you as he
Will piece up in himself.

William Shakespeare, *The Winter's Tale*

SIXPENNY WOODS on the border of Wiltshire and Dorset is a stretch of road passing through dark woodland that has been the site of several fatal car accidents over the course of the last few decades. It is also believed to be inhabited by a ghost. Survivors of road accidents on that stretch have reported seeing a woman rush out from between the trees as they were driving, as if to throw herself in front of them, causing them to swerve and lose control of their vehicles. All of these people have reported that by the time their cars had become stationary, the woman was nowhere to be seen. The story has grown up as a result of these strange sightings that the wood is haunted by a woman who wishes to lure people in among the trees with her, so that she will be less alone; a woman who appears out of nowhere to shock passers-by into stopping their journey and keeping her company. What the reality of the situation is, no one knows. It may be that the shadows cast by those trees play particular tricks; or that a woman lives near there intent on causing mischief; or that a woman lives near there who is badly unbalanced, and looking for help; or it may even be that the woods are haunted by a ghost who just doesn't want to be alone any more.

AMNESIA. The dance of forgetting. The loss of things. The displacement of identity. The confirmation of the suspicion you held all your life that the world is a dream, like a fog gathered round you – a suspicion finally proven when the fog unthreads itself, leaving you grasping at the ghost of it.

WALLED GARDENS. After my dad left, my mum had no one. Though we tried, I don't think my brother or sister or I could ever have been an adequate replacement. The closeness a parent has with their child is not the same closeness you have with the person you share your bed with, your secret life. Not better or worse, just different, in ways that can never be reconciled. Sometimes I would attempt to play both roles and it placed a strange and alienating pressure on me. Sometimes it felt like Mum wanted too much, because every day I came home and she needed to hear all of me, and then she needed to give me the whole story of her day, unburden herself by talking. I regret very deeply that it wasn't a weight I could really bear, that I couldn't help her more.

Once I'd moved away from home, I visited when I could, but never got close to her again, never felt like I really broke through to talking with her unguardedly. She walled herself into her cottage in the country, in the middle of nowhere, walled herself into a life that didn't need anyone else. What that amounted to, it seemed to me, was a kind of half-life, in which the price of coping with being alone was never to let in any emotion, keeping all that she felt at arm's length. When she was dying, the worst thing she went through was that everyone insisted on visiting. She told me once how she would sit in her cottage dreading the bell or the knock or the phone, the last hello, the catch-up call. She couldn't stand the feelings they all brought in with them, like mud on the bottom of their boots.

I knew exactly what Mum hated about the kindness people showed her in the year she was dying. I had lived the same thing for myself, spent my hours trying to disappear completely. And I knew first hand that it didn't work: nothing was numbed by living in abeyance; nothing was ever felt less keenly. It did no good to wall yourself away from things – in the end it was only a fear of life. That was what I knew had really happened to both of us. We pretended we were protecting ourselves. In fact we were frightened and living half-lives. Like mother, like daughter.

After Mum died, I thought back over my life, and thinking about her helped me see what had happened to me as well. Scalded by the world, we'd both shied away from it. That had cursed us into experiencing life as little more than a pause before dying. An exile until we could go home. And I felt as if my heart would break, because it seemed to be too late to do anything about it.

TRANSIENT GLOBAL AMNESIA. A specific displacement of memory where an individual regresses, in perfect detail, to a previous date in their life, believing themselves to be alive once again on that date, and recovering and feeling once again the pressures and ambitions of that moment. If a mind can flit from year to year, might it be possible for the right jolt to cast it into different bodies too?

I listened with growing amazement as the stranger sitting opposite me told his tale. At first I was carried away with what he said, caught up in his voice and following each turn of his story.

He seemed to be dreaming some extraordinary adventure, and it was exciting to watch him pull the next story out of the air. But as he went on, I was slowly stripped of the certainty that what I was hearing had really happened. I started to doubt whether this strange, lost man was getting his story right.

The more I listened to the story as he told it, the more I wondered whether any part could really be true. It wasn't possible, after all – what he described could never have physically happened, and so I felt sure that he wasn't just breathing life back into what he had seen. He was creating. The tale was pocked with inconsistencies. Nothing he was telling me was real at all. I felt like I had heard parts of it before, and as he went on, I started dimly to remember having come across a story in a newspaper about a cannabis farm that was found in Wiltshire, run by children locked in there who had been trafficked all the way from Vietnam. And I remembered a story about a taxi driver in Swindon who had taken young women out to the woods. And a story about a brother and sister who had taken the ashes of their parents and jumped from the Dover cliffs, because no one would help them, and they did not know how to tell anyone the trouble they were in. Could he have been reading the same articles? Could he have been spinning his story from there, disguising other lives as his own, or perhaps not really knowing where one ended and the other began, perhaps sliding from one into the other in the slopes and wilds of his imagination? That must be what he was doing. None of this could really have happened to him.

And yet I knew with a cold and vertiginous certainty that for all that these tragedies couldn't really have happened quite as he said, the story he was telling me was true. Because the thing was – and I could barely believe it, but it wasn't long before

I accepted it had to be true – the thing was that I was the woman he had left behind. I was the wife he had never come home to.

I didn't know quite what to do when I realised my part in the story, where I ought to look, and whether I ought to tell him. He avoided my eyes for most of the time he spoke, lost in memory – should I interrupt him? I didn't feel I could. I didn't know what I was feeling. Too many emotions were at war in my head.

It was shocking and strange to recognise myself in his story, like stepping into a dream, but there I was all the same, falling once more into the argument that had decided so much of my life, losing the person who I had thought to build a life around once again. It was shocking to look at the grey man opposite me and remember the young man I had known, and then as he spoke to see traces of his former self, echoes of the man who disappeared. The man I had loved. I felt sick, and afraid, and excited; I felt shocked and betrayed and enraged.

I grew up a few miles south of the pub where we were sitting, then left Wiltshire for London when I finished school to try and make my way into the world. It was shortly after this that I met the man I was sitting opposite now. Things took the course they do among the young – we fell into bed, and fell in love, whatever that means, and a few years later we found ourselves marrying and embarking on a life together. A shared dream. I was twenty-one and I thought the world would last for ever.

'Will there be children?' I remember asking, while we lay in bed one night in each other's arms.

'Do you want there to be?'

'More than anything.'

He smiled.

'Then there'll be children.'

'How many?'

'How many do you want?'

'I don't know. Not one. One is lonely.'

'So two.'

'Or three. Two might be lonely as well.'

'Do you think so?' He seemed surprised, and moved to look at me, propping himself up on one elbow.

'I think two could still be lonely.'

'Do you ever feel lonely with me?'

'Sometimes.'

'Why?'

'I don't know. Do you never feel lonely with me?' I wondered whether I had said something strange, something wrong. But then he smiled.

'If only.'

'What does that mean!'

'You never bloody leave me alone.'

'That's not fair!'

'I wish I had time to feel lonely.'

'You'll have plenty if you go on like that.'

We didn't talk for a while then. Our hands were on each other's bodies, legs entwined. We lay and experienced the heat of each other, feeling close together.

'It's good to be lonely sometimes, I think,' he said.

'Yes?'

'That's when you think about things.'

'Not too often though.'

'No.'

'Or you'd never have anyone to talk to about the things you thought.'

It seemed like we had so much time to talk and lie in the arms of one another, but it ended so quickly instead. By the time I was twenty-five, I was on my own again, and the decades passed since then have shown me another side of life. The colder shoulder.

The man I married, the man I was listening to over a glass of wine now in The Bear, was an actor when I met him, and crippled and half-mad with ambition, just as he described it in the story that he told. I was impressed, listening to him, with the depth of his self-knowledge. He hadn't had any the last time I'd seen him.

LEAP. The last act of someone desperate. The first act of someone brave. Often both things at the same time, if you look closely.

I spent that first night of his disappearance angry and upset, certain he had gone to the pub and met some woman and gone home with her to try and hurt me. It wasn't till the following evening that I started feeling afraid. I came home from work and noticed that he had been back to the flat. He had taken a bag of clothes, a second pair of shoes – it seemed that he would be away for a while, then. This was in the days before mobile phones, of course, so the only way I could think to contact him was calling up his agent the next morning when their offices opened. The embarrassed man who looked after my husband's career listened to my story about the fight, and the two nights we had now spent apart, and the bag of clothes he had taken away with him, and said he would pass a message on as soon as my husband got in touch. A few days later, I received a letter. *Don't try to contact me. I'm not in a place to talk right now.*

After that, I was on my own.

He filed for divorce a few months later, sending the legal papers to the flat with a covering note: *We did the wrong thing; I haven't got room for anyone else. I know that's my failing, but it's true all the same and I've realised I can't change it. My darling, my heart's too small, I'm sorry.* By that time there was another man sleeping in the flat with me, because I'd wanted someone near me, feeling so badly on my own, and he offered to track my husband down and kick his head in. But I told him to leave it. I signed the forms. Things rumbled on between our solicitors, brown envelopes, and then after a trawl of time had passed, a letter came to say that it was finished. The shocking, sharp-edged clarity with which he had severed our lives made me certain there was no accident in this, and that there was to be no persuading. He felt he had made a mistake, and in the light of that, all I could think of for us to do was try to get away from each other. I wrote to let him know that I would start the process of selling the flat, and that I would take my half of the money from it, as was my right. He didn't argue with that. Four months after we last saw each other, I packed all my things into boxes and moved back to Wiltshire, and here I have been ever since.

I was devastated at first. I felt numb and emptied with the shock of someone wanting to get rid of me, and being able to do it as easily as that. Just like what had happened to me at the beginning of my story. I hadn't seen it coming at all. Of course, the arguing made me unhappy, but I thought all couples argued, and when I talked to other women I knew at work, they agreed that everyone did. But I think they must have meant a different kind of argument. I think they must never have imagined the way we used to live. That's the only explanation I can come up with for how things fell apart – we may have thought we were struggling to fit together like other people, but really our struggles were much worse, much more desperate.

In the first year after he left me, I felt I could see quite quickly the path I might take if I chose to lose my mind over what had happened. Another strange phrase that one, to 'lose your mind', because it's the whole of you that gets lost, not any one part, when you slip into grief, into madness. I saw well enough how that could happen. A few more drinks here and there, a shutting-away from other people, shutting myself up, a little obsession over the way things had been and not the world around me now and I could quite easily have lost touch with the real world before very long. There were times when I started to let it happen to me. But I could see a route out of things as well. The chance to get over my divorce and my false start, and move on with my life and find some happiness. I couldn't have been in love after all, whatever that meant; I must have been too young to really know what was happening, and rushed things, and missed turnings. It must have been earlier that I was lost, and this was my chance to get back on track. I worked very hard at believing that I had never quite been in love.

And who can say I ever had been? What do those words even mean? In time, I came to believe there was nothing to mourn, that there had never been anything real between us at all. I told myself that love is a verb, the continual sharing of oneself with another person who is there with you, who is active in your life. It is something that is always happening now, not in the memory; it is now. If that was true then I couldn't be in love. And if that was true then I couldn't be in the pain I was in. By such reasoning, I found ways to imagine the pain out of sight. I couldn't be in love. Except with the birds who gathered outside my window; except with the light through the blinds in the morning; except with the things around me and present and immediate each day, right now. So time passed, and I started to get over him. Time passed, and there were bumps in the road, and I suppose a layman would quibble with the idea that I never fell victim to any kind of madness, because over the years I have had a bit to do with psychiatrists; I have had a fair bit to do with hospitals. But the thing is that I got better. I climbed out of the pit I felt I'd been cast into, and got my bungalow, and pulled together a sort of life, and I was proud of that. That was enough for me.

In the long years since he had left me, he had flitted in and out of the edge of my life from time to time. I would see him on the TV, or hear his voice in a radio play, and find myself carried back to that false start in London, the years when I had thought my life was growing, but then had to throw away as if they'd never happened. It would shake me; I found it upsetting to think about what he'd done with the rest of his life, all that time I had thought I might be part of. But in the end his career didn't turn out the way he would have wanted it, like most people's don't, and so over time I heard less and less of him, as the work dried up.

On this day, the day we met again, I think it had been years since I had caught any sight of him, though it seemed his path through time might perhaps have involved a few psychiatrists and hospitals as well. He was entirely delusional, lost in a dream of his own making. I had met plenty of people like that over the years, in waiting rooms and treatment rooms. I wondered whether he, too, was in The Bear today because he'd had an appointment at Green Lanes. I listened and felt as if the ground were falling away from under me. My body was alive and burning at the thought that he was sitting here, speaking of all this. I felt emotional and frightened, like someone in a nightmare, like someone in the grip of a dream.

What I didn't know, and wanted desperately to understand, was whether he was telling me this story because he knew who I was. Whether he had opened up his heart like this by way of a disguised apology or explanation, or whether he didn't know me at all and was simply talking, confessing, filling the air. I watched his face for clues while he spoke, but he didn't look at me often. His concentration was focused on getting the words out, giving this account of himself. I could see it was difficult for him, and took all his strength. When his eyes flicked up from time to time to meet mine, they had a hunted and guarded look. Of course, he was used to not being believed, he was used to being laughed at. But I couldn't tell whether he knew who I was. It was painful to believe he might not recognise me, but I couldn't be sure. When he finished telling his story and sat back in his chair, sighing deeply as if speaking had left him feeling the weight of a great loss, I didn't know how to find out what he knew and what he hadn't yet realised.

RECOVER. To save or rescue something. To grow back a skin that can shelter nerve endings. To be able to feel again without the feeling burning. To bloom again, to sprout new life, put roots down. To have gone through hell.

'That's an extraordinary story,' I said to him.
He smiled.
'It's all right. No one ever believes it.'
'I didn't say I didn't believe it. I just mean you've been through a very great deal.'
'So you believe it?'
'I think there would be different ways of believing it, wouldn't there?'
'How do you mean?'
'Well, you must have thought about this over the years. You'll understand it much better than me. But the way we experience things, that's not always the whole truth, is it? That doesn't mean

it isn't true, if it's the way we feel them, but there's often other truths to be told as well, aren't there?'

He nodded at this, and I could see in the light in his eyes that he was excited, that he had expected me to laugh at him for what he'd said, and it gave him hope that I hadn't. It gave him hope that he could maybe believe in himself, if he could make someone else believe in him.

'I think you're right there.'

'So your life may not have looked like you say it did to other people, to passers-by. But that doesn't mean it didn't look that way to you.'

'I think you're just right about that.'

'You're not used to people listening to that story all the way through, are you?'

He laughed.

'No one wants to listen to folk like me, no. It makes people uncomfortable. Because if they're not careful, they worry they could end up like me one day.'

'How do you mean?'

'Seeing through a cracked lens. And drinking in the day.'

'I'm drinking in the day.'

'Yeah, but wine – wine's a classier way to get drunk.'

We both smiled at that.

'Is that how you see it? You think you're seeing through a cracked lens?'

'I think everyone is.'

'How do you mean?'

'No one sees the whole world. No one sees things as they really are. They see their own versions of it.'

'Do you think?'

'Do you listen to jazz music?'

'A bit. Not really.'

'Imagine the world is the greatest song ever written. I don't know which one – imagine the world is "My Funny Valentine", something like that. Now, in jazz, no one ever claims there's any such thing as a definitive version of "My Funny Valentine", do they? There are only different people's versions, and that's just fine, that's what people expect, because that's the way jazz is. No one ever plays the whole of "My Funny Valentine" and gets to the end of it, wraps it all up. It will never end, because there'll always be someone else about to come along who's going to play it different. I think that's how the world is, too. There's no reason there should be any one sure final way of looking at it. I think the world is just everyone in it, playing out their own version, and never getting all the way to the end.'

'I see.'

'The thing in jazz, the thing people who listen to jazz look for, is intentionality. You heard that word?'

'No.'

'It's like – it's like your attack, I suppose. Have you got a way of cutting into "My Funny Valentine", an angle. I'm not putting that well. Do you know what I mean?'

'It's your take on things.'

'Yeah. Sort of, yeah. But you can have a take on things that's wishy-washy and doesn't know what it thinks. If you have intentionality, you know what you think.'

'And you think that's what you have about your life, you think you have intentionality?'

He roared with laughter, taking me by surprise.

'No, no. I think no one ever had less. I was just going to say I think that's what I lost, in the long ago. And I think it's what everyone's looking for as well.'

'Oh, I see. I see what you were saying now.'

He leaned forward in his chair and fixed me with a look, and I wondered whether this was the moment he was going to come clean with me, admit he had remembered who I was.

'I lost the trick of having shape to things. So all I've known how to do for the last however many years is hold on to my hat while I got pinballed from one day round to another, and sometimes back again, and sometimes missing out dozens at a time. I know for lots of people, life is more joined up than I find it; they have plans that they see through, and the same characters turn up in all the scenes of their lives. Whereas in mine, I barely ever see anyone ever again. I only meet mayflies. And you think that would be fun, maybe, just to be with people for a moment and then dance away from them again, because everything would always be now, everything would always be new, but it's not quite like that in reality. Because no one really lets you in the first time you meet them. I never get close to anyone. Not for a long time, not since I last saw my wife. I never know what anyone's thinking, and no one ever finds out about me. God knows the last time I told anyone this much of my story – you're kind to listen. Even though I know the next time one of us walks out of this room, I'll be carried away to a different world.'

'How do you think you could change how things feel for you?'

'I think if there was any way of doing that, I missed my chance of finding it a long, long time ago. Unless, I suppose, unless I found my way back to the story I was starting out on when the whole thing went wrong.'

I felt a sickness in my stomach then, heat in my palms, on my cheeks, my blood racing.

'What story do you mean?'

'Well, the story of my wife I never got back to. But the trouble is, there's no going back to any time, not really. No one ever gets back to anything once it's gone. Because she won't have stayed frozen in that flat waiting for me. I know that. I have to accept it. She isn't still thinking I might be out there. This was all years ago, you remember. She moved on a whole lifetime ago, and she wouldn't want to hear from me.'

I felt my heart sink. So he didn't remember me. He didn't know who I was. He'd told all that story simply because he needed to let it out of him. I wondered why that upset me as much as it did. Surely he was right, surely I ought to have moved on long ago, and never wanted to hear from him again? But we were sitting here talking, and I couldn't help feeling that this was what had always been wrong, this was the thing I'd never got control of. He had never come home all my life, and I had missed him all that time, I had been waiting for him, even if I had forgotten it or hidden it from myself.

ALONE. A place where no one can reach you, so the world is briefly bearable. A place where no one can reach you, so the world is briefly unbearable. Everyone alive is on their own island. Everyone alive is adrift at sea trying to make landfall, anywhere, anywhere.

It made me feel ashamed to think like that. Was it stupid to feel the loss like this? Should I be embarrassed? Perhaps it wasn't so weak or strange to ache for a love that had never quite bloomed. We had married one another, after all. And to stand at the altar and say those words, and mean them, and then for that marriage to come to an end, perhaps that would put the halters on someone in a way that would mean they

185

never recovered. But it felt very shameful to me sitting there, to think I'd been trapped in that beat of my heart ever since he went away.

'Maybe you're right,' I said. 'Maybe she wouldn't want to speak to you now. Maybe it wouldn't be good for either of you.'

'Well yes, exactly. I don't think it does people all that much good to let themselves get whirlpooled back into their pasts too much. People ought to get used to the fact that they're going to keep going forwards. Until they can't go forwards any more.'

'Yes.'

He looked down into the empty glass before him.

'I appear to have finished my drink.'

'Will you have another?'

'That's kind of you, but I shouldn't. I have a long way to travel, I think.'

'Where are you going?'

He shrugged.

'I don't know. I never know, you see. I just think it will be a long way, and usually it is. Everywhere always feels like a long way, because everywhere else has always disappeared by the time I get to where I'm going. Everywhere I've ever been feels like the only island in the world once I'm in it, and I always feel like I've had to swim all the way to it.'

'I see. So how will it happen? You'll walk out of that door and then you'll be in a different world?'

'I think so, yes. That's how it usually happens.'

'And even if I were to follow straight after you, you wouldn't be there any more?'

'That's the way it's always gone for me. Whenever I turn my back on anyone, I never know if I'm going to see them again.'

'That must be very hard.'

'The good thing is that I never have enough time to get attached to any one person. So the only pain is the pain of being alone, and that doesn't hurt as sharp as the pain of losing a particular someone.'

'I suppose that's good news, then.'

'I'd rather I didn't have either, of course, but I think I have the better pain.'

'Except of course you have the pain of never having found your way back to your wife.'

'Yes, I have that. But when that comes, I just tell myself that she forgot me long ago. And then it gets more bearable, if I can persuade myself I'm only alone, not apart from anyone.'

He pushed back his chair abruptly as if to stand, as if to get away from me.

'Are you all right?' I said.

'I shouldn't have taken so much of your time. It only gets me upset to talk about it.'

'Why does it upset you?'

'Who wouldn't feel heartbroken thinking over the way they can't have any of their life again?'

He was standing now, and I realised I was losing him; I was about to lose him if I didn't say something. But fear stopped my tongue. I didn't know how to tell him what I was feeling. Perhaps I didn't know what I was feeling well enough to be able to say it aloud.

'Time to go?' I asked him.

'You'll need to get home to your dinner and all.'

'I suppose so. It doesn't take ever so long to put a meal in a microwave, though.'

'All the same, I've kept you too long.'

I bowed my head. He had become agitated and wanted to leave, and there seemed no point in trying to stop him.

'All right then. It was good to meet you.'

'And you. I don't know the last time someone listened to my story. I'm grateful to you, you're kind.'

'It's not kindness. You tell a good story.'

He smiled.

'Maybe I do. Didn't feel so good at the time, though.'

Then he bowed his head to me, a strangely formal gesture, and turned and opened the door of the pub, and then he was gone.

I sat in shock, and I didn't know what had just happened, and I didn't know how I could have let it happen. Had he really just left again? Was this real or was it some kind of dreaming? Had I found him after all this time, only to let him go? I hadn't had a chance to work out what I wanted. There hadn't been time. Part of me thought there could be nothing worse than letting a ghost like that one back into my life after so very long – and yet what are our lives but the themes that rise up out of them? And hadn't he once been half my life? Shouldn't I have told him who I was, and seen what happened, and let the story grow? It is so cruel that we must all get through this life with no script to lead us.

Had there been other men I had wanted to be close to, in the years since I had lost this man? Yes, from time to time. But none had lasted. I had never felt serious enough about any of them to want to put real roots down, to want to have children, and in the end that had meant I'd ended up alone. Had there been other centres, other meanings to who I had been in the years since, besides this relationship I had hoped to place at the heart of my life? Of course there had been – but what did they amount to now I thought my way back over them, like so many rocks in the sea's chopping shallows? I had performed various roles in various companies, I had been there for friends, I had taken lovers, I had made one home after another. But had any of them been any more than the building of sandcastles? The dredging together of reasons to stay alive? In the moment I was sitting in now, I couldn't quite believe that any of them had amounted to much. All of them felt like nothing more than screens I had tried to place between me and the end of the world, which had lasted for a little while, but never really lasted long. They had had no true heft to them. They had all been burned up before long in the heat given off by the approach of the end of the world, the end of my life. And perhaps that was the way all meanings came to an end, I don't know – but in this moment, plunged so suddenly back into the life I had thought I might have had once with this man, I couldn't help but feel as if there had once been a real life, a true story I might have lived, and that for a moment I had been given a glimpse of how to get back to it. Could that be true? Was this the world showing me a chance of getting home? And had I just let it go, let it walk out the door? Had I elected to remain in the dark, drifting outside for ever?

I stood up from my chair, head spinning, feeling possessed, propelled by an energy that barely seemed to be mine. I didn't know what I wanted. I didn't know what was wise. But all the same, I walked across the floor of the bar till I came to the front door and took hold of the handle, because I was alive, I was alive, I was alive for a little while longer, and the way we spend each minute as we lose it will end up being the story we lived, and in the end, I may get things wrong, I may let things slip, but what I could not bear would be to die and there never to have been a story. For me never to have taken a step. I got to the door and opened the door and looked out through it, and in the cold of the winter street, there he was, still standing with his back turned to me. I could see him shivering. I could see the tension written over his body. Slowly, he turned to look at me standing there in the doorway, and I realised he could see the same tension and the same shivers passing through me as well.

'Am I still here?' he asked me.

'You are,' I said.

'Can you still see me?'

'I can.'

'I haven't gone into a different world.'

'You haven't.'

'Have they let me stop travelling? Have they let me come home?'

'Who are they? There's no one doing anything. There's only us, isn't there – look around.'

He looked around him, tentative.

'I thought you didn't recognise me,' he said.

Electric charges seemed to pass through my whole body, through my stomach, through my spine.

'Do you know who I am?' I asked.

'I thought you didn't know me.'

'I thought the same.'

'I tried to tell you. That was why I told you the story. I was trying to tell you I know I let you down.'

I understood then. I saw the way he had been trying to reach for me. I saw the way he had searched for the words.

'Why didn't you just say?'

'I got used long ago to the thought that I'd never see you again. I would keep travelling for ever, but I'd never find you. I didn't know how to shake the thought away. I didn't know how to deserve you.'

I walked towards him then, and took his hands in mine, and we stood for a moment in silence and looked at each other.

I could see the young man trapped behind the eyes of this old body stood before me. I could see my real life just beneath the surface of this scene I was in. I could feel my heart beating like it was breaking through the wall of my chest. For so long I had been trying to get back to the time when the world went right. And this man had been the closest I ever came to recovering that lost balance, that lost order to things. He had been the closest I had ever come to feeling allowed to breathe out again, and let go of all the guilt and shame I had carried with me, and live in the world without fearing I didn't deserve it. He had seemed, for a moment, to offer me some equilibrium. Then he had gone, and I had gone searching for other masks worth wearing, and I'd never found any. And now here he was again. It was too much to take in. I couldn't see any further than the scene we were in, to the way this might change the rest of my life.

'Is it really you?' I asked him.

'It is.'

'Did you really want to come home to me?'

'All this time.'

'You really changed your mind?'

'I got it wrong, my love. I got it wrong.'

I looked at him. I didn't know how to tell him. I didn't know how to put into words this thing I was feeling.

'What are we going to do now?' I said. 'What are we going to do if you've come home?'

The street was trying to freeze us. He looked over my shoulder at the door to The Bear.

'Do you want to go back inside and talk? I've talked so much. I'd like to listen to you.'

And I was ready to begin. However difficult it was to find the words, I felt sure that I wanted to. Because someone wanted to listen to me. So we turned and walked into The Bear together, knowing as we did that when we passed through that doorway, we would enter into a different world.

Acknowledgements

Thanks are due to Charlie, Alice, Peter Tyas and Wiltshire County Council, Robert Shea-Simonds, the Richmond Fellowship at Green Lane in Devizes and all who recover there, and to Mark Powell, Gareth Machin and Salisbury Playhouse, all of whom organised and shared with me over many years the workshops and visits that led to this writing. Crucially, Alice also introduced me to the paintings of David Inshaw, which have profoundly energised my work.

Thanks to Laura Williams, Suzanne Bridson, Alice Youell, Claire Gatzen, Sophie Christopher, James Jones and everyone at Peters Fraser and Dunlop, Greene & Heaton and Transworld Books.

Thanks are also due to Shep, whose love of Devizes only added to its allure. 'Have you heard the news?'

There are stories here which draw on truth. The source stories behind this book snagged my attention and I share them here for the same reason I have always written – to implore us all to care.

Thanks to my family, for sharing so much of the world in this book with me.

Above all this is a story about recovery, and I would like to add my thanks to the Priory in Woking, the Bethlem Royal Hospital, Frank and Elizabeth Brenan, Dad and Joanna Mersey, who supported the treatment that has allowed Charlie and me to face the world with new determination.

March on, march on, since we are up in arms ...

BARNEY NORRIS was born in Sussex in 1987. Upon leaving university, he founded the touring theatre company Up In Arms. He won the Critics' Circle Award for Most Promising Playwright for his debut full-length play *Visitors*; his other plays include *Nightfall*, which appeared in the inaugural season of the Bridge Theatre, and an acclaimed adaptation of Kazuo Ishiguro's *The Remains of the Day*. He is the Martin Esslin Playwright in Residence at Keble College, Oxford, a Fellow of the Royal Society of Literature, and has been named by the *Evening Standard* as one of the 1,000 Most Influential Londoners.

He is the author of *Turning for Home* and the critically acclaimed *Five Rivers Met on a Wooded Plain*, which was a *Times* bestseller and won a Betty Trask award. It was also shortlisted for the Ondaatje Prize and Debut of the Year at the British Book Awards. *The Vanishing Hours* is his third novel.